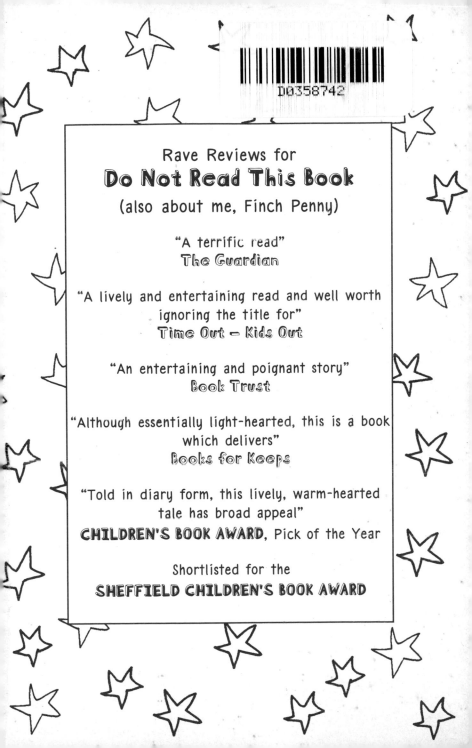

Rave Reviews for
Do Not Read This Book
(also about me, Finch Penny)

"A terrific read"
The Guardian

"A lively and entertaining read and well worth
ignoring the title for"
Time Out – Kids Out

"An entertaining and poignant story"
Book Trust

"Although essentially light-hearted, this is a book
which delivers"
Books for Keeps

"Told in diary form, this lively, warm-hearted
tale has broad appeal"
CHILDREN'S BOOK AWARD, Pick of the Year

Shortlisted for the
SHEFFIELD CHILDREN'S BOOK AWARD

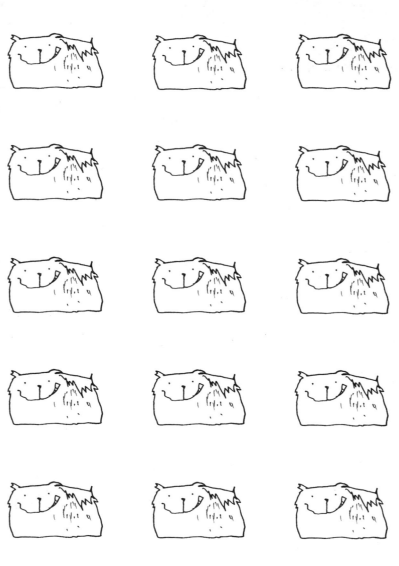

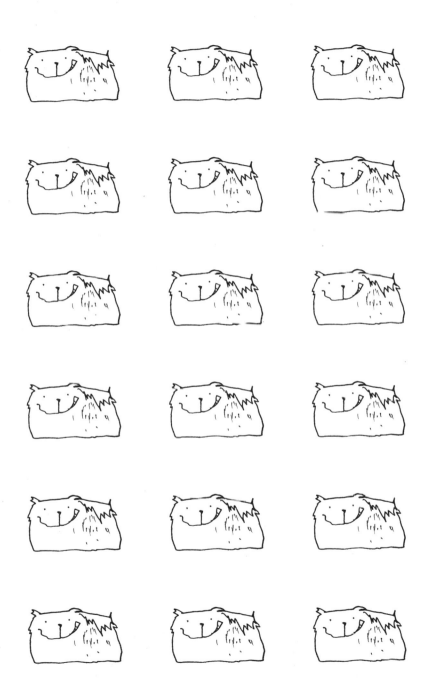

With thanks to Rory, Jill, Zoe and Howard
Hilton and Nigel the rabbit, for all I needed
to know about rabbits.

DO NOT READ ANY FURTHER

Part Two of FINCH'S TOP SECRETS* ON

Boys
Rabbits
Warrior princesses
School
Guinea pigs
Friends
Enemies
Worry bugs
Cringeworld
Kissing
Bullies
Socks
Teachers
Sleepovers
Babies
Slagging-off world
Wrinklies
Etcetera

*As revealed only to Pat Moon

☆ STOP! ☆

DO NOT read any further!
DO NOT try to sneak!
DON'T even try to take a peek!
These are **MY** secrets!
And **MINE** alone.
So just **BUZZ OFF!**
And write your own!

☆ ☆ ☆

WARNING!

Black belt bunny

BLACK BELT
BUNNYGUARD
ON DUTY AT
ALL TIMES

🌸 THIS BOOK BELONGS TO 🌸

Finch Olive Penny

HAIR – Long and dark brown.
EYES – Green.
HEIGHT – 167.5 cms.

WHAT I LIKE ABOUT MYSELF
Hair and eyes.
WHAT I HATE ABOUT MYSELF
My spindly legs. Wearing glasses.

AGE when I started this book of my life:
twelve years, seven weeks and six days.

MY FAMILY:

Mum: Debbie Penny. She's a care assistant at Greytiles Home For Wrinklies.

Dad: Tom Someone – who my mum met at a party and never saw again. She was only seventeen when she had me! I think she was very brave to have me all on her own.

Gran: Olive McKay (she's Scottish) but me and Mum call her Nolly. This is because I couldn't say Nanna Olive properly when I was little – it came out sounding like Nolly. We're not really related, but just before I was born Mum moved in with Nolly and after I was born she became my adopted gran.

We all live at: Nolly's House: 51 Nelson Street, Fletchley.

MY BEST FRIENDS:

Cassandra Owens
(known as Cassie or Cass) because...
We've been best friends since
we met at playgroup when
we were three.
We have the same sense of
humour.
We are dead opposites, which
makes it REALLY interesting.
We look after each other...
BUT...she's going to a different school next
term! It's going to be S☉ weird not sitting
next to her in class − after nine years
together! I'm really going to MISS her!

Graeme Penny because...
He's the world's most intelligent
rabbit. I tell him all my secrets
and can trust him not to tell
ANY☉NE. Sometimes it seems
as if he can read my mind! He
can always tell whether I'm sad
or happy. He makes me laugh.

Jay Carter!
I met him on the visit to my new school,
Fletchley High. We will be in the same tutor
group. I have known him for exactly five
weeks and four days. (Finch + Jay = Bird
buddies! Ha ha!) He is DREAMY!

9

Sunday, 22nd August

10.00. This is Book Two of MY LIFE. Cannot believe that I've filled a **WHOLE BOOK** already! At the start of Book One it was just me, Mum, Nolly and Graeme. BUT NOW...

1. MUM'S GOT A BOYFRIEND! Old Action Man Swively-eyes Ian Tanner. He came to repair the washing machine and now he's here every day. I hated him SO MUCH at first that I made out he'd hit me so that Mum would get rid of him. It worked too and Mum sent him packing. But afterwards she went all depressed so I confessed. I admit that I was a **TOTAL BRAT!** I still go all cringey just thinking about it.

2. I'VE GOT A BOYFRIEND! **Jay!** We're going to sit together when we start at Fletchley High, though we haven't been out together, just the two of us, yet.

3. CASSIE AND ME ARE BEING SPLIT UP because her pushy mum is forcing her to go to

posh St Monica's School for Girls. We are
DEVASTATED.
4. NOLLY'S IN HOSPITAL recovering from a
heart attack.
SO...what does the future hold, I wonder.

1. Will Ian stay Mum's boyfriend?
2. How will I manage without Cassie?
3. How will Cassie manage without me?
4. Will Nolly...
            (a) be OK after her heart attack?
OR   **(b)** Will she go back to her ciggies?
5. Will I ever move on from a size 32A bra?
BY THE END OF THIS BOOK I SHALL KNOW
ALL THE ANSWERS! **THAT IS SO SPOOKY!!!!!**

11.05. I've got a huge spot – right on
the top of my nose! It sort of glows
and makes me go cross-eyed looking
at it. I will cheer myself up by
writing...

My New Wish List
1. *I wish that my spot would
disappear.*
2. *I wish that Nolly will be well enough to
come home from hospital soon.*
3. *I wish she doesn't have any more heart
attacks.*
4. *I wish that she doesn't start smoking
again.*

5. I wish that I get on OK at my new school, *Fletchley High.* Last term Kayleigh promised I could go round with her and Carmen, but I'm going to feel so lonesome without Cass.

6. I wish that Cassie's mum sees how cruel it is to split us up and lets Cass come to Fletchley High with me.

OR...

7. I wish that Graeme picks the winning Lotto numbers, then I can go to St Mon's too.

8. I wish that Mum lets me have one of Jay's baby guinea pigs as a prezzie for Graeme on his fourth birthday next week... He would LOVE a hutch-buddy!

9. I wish I knew what to say to Ian. It's so squirm-making when he's being all matey with me and it really winds me up. And why does he have to be so bouncy all the time? He's driving me bananas!

On my last **WISH LIST** five out of my seventeen wishes came **TRUE!**

1. Nolly stopped smoking. (Because of her heart attack and doctor's orders.)

2. My chest is growing! It is now 82 cms. That's 3.5 cms since my birthday on 28th June. So long as it doesn't grow as big as Cassie's. Her's is ginormous. But she's nearly thirteen. She gets really embarrassed and covers up with baggy tops all the time.

3. The annoying Shane Ripley will not be in my class.
4. Mum told me the truth about my dad instead of pretending he'd died.
5. At my new school I am going to sit next to someone really nice — Jay! He's so YUM-YUM!

12.30. Going round to Cassie's now. She only got back from holiday on Friday and I haven't told her yet about how I lied to Mum that Ian had hit me. Cassie and me tell each other everything. I think I'll feel a bit better after that. I couldn't feel much worse.

16.00. Cassie's mum is doing a Beautician Course. She got all excited about my glowing nose because she could use it to test some special new spot patches. She's got loads of lotions and creams and stuff, so we did **Beauty Salon.** On went the face packs, and some cucumber slices for our eyes, and we lay on Cassie's bed. Cassie played this really relaxing CD of her mum's — all sorts of shushing sea sounds, like being on a beautiful desert island — and then I told Cass about those **HUGE PORKIES** I'd told about Ian. (Not that I actually TOLD huge porkies to Mum. I just wrote them in

13

my diary, then left it lying around for her to find.) Cassie was so shocked that she shot bolt upright and her cucumber slices fell off. She blinked at me, *What! You mean you made your mum believe that Ian hit you! Wow! You really did **hate** him, didn't you! Wow wow, wow!* She went on about it a bit too much, actually. Then she said, *But, you did own up, that's what matters.* I feel a bit better now that I've told her. Her mum gave me a box of spot patches.

21.00. Ian's been here all day. We've been swapping over Mum's and Nolly's flats for when Nolly comes home from hospital. Nolly will have our old flat downstairs and Mum and me will have Nolly's old one upstairs, except my bedroom will stay downstairs, next to Nolly's. I've been helping Mum and Ian paint Nolly's old flat. It stank of ciggies! They kept fooling about and dabbing each other with paint and laughing hysterically. You'd think they were infants.

21.25. Graeme has made a nest in my old school bag under my desk. He looks so dinky. I've put some straw in for him. He's such a good house bunny.

Monday, 23rd August
8.45. I woke up in a really **HAPPY** mood

because I had this
amazing dream that
Graeme grew wings!
They were these
lovely silky, white
furry-feather wings,
all pink underneath.

And either I'd shrunk — or he'd grown
ENORMOUS, because I climbed onto his back
and off we flew. First we went to Jay's house
— and he climbed on too. Then we flew off to
Cassie's house — but she was mad with me
because I'd gone to Jay's first. She cheered up
once she'd climbed on, and we flew higher
and higher, right above the clouds — and then
I woke up. I wonder if rabbits dream.

9.15. The spot patch was brilliant. The spot's
gone all shrively!

THINGS TO DO THIS WEEK

Graeme's Fourth Birthday Party
1. Keep nagging Mum to let me have one of
Jay's baby guinea pigs as a birthday prezzie
for Graeme. PLEEEEEEZE! She keeps saying
that she's got more important things to
think about than guinea pigs. Yeah, I know.
Like Ian!
2. Deliver invites to Cassie, Jay, his mate
Dan, also Kayleigh and Carmen from school.

Graeme's friend Smiffy, the guinea pig next door, can't come after all because he's got dire-reah.

3. Make a treasure hunt game for Graeme.
4. Organise some food and drinks.

16.30. Asked Graeme if he'd like a little baby guinea piggy hutch-buddy for his birthday. He ran round and round in circles squeaking, *Yes! Yes! Yes!*

It's weird being in the house all on my own. Now that Mum's back at work at Greytiles Home for Wrinklies, there's only Graeme and me here. I miss having Nolly around loads.

Tuesday, 24th August
10.05. WORRY LIST

WHAT IF...
1. Nolly has another heart attack?
2. I HATE Fletchley High School?
3. I don't make friends? Kayleigh and Carmen are OK—ish. But it won't be the same as having a best friend. Also Kayleigh borrows stuff and never gives it back. She's still got my pink hair mascara.
4. Cassie makes friends with all those rich girls at her new school and doesn't want to know me any more?

5. What if...
THIS IS STUPID! I must give myself a good talking to.

PULL YOURSELF TOGETHER!
OK! I WILL!

Graeme has just dived under the bed. Think I'm going bonkers.
WISH 10 *I wish Nolly were home.*
WISH 11 *I wish I could stop worrying.*

10.50. Cassie phoned. She can't come round 'cos her Mum's got a migraine so she's got to look after Leo, her little pest of a brother.

21.30. Ian here all evening. He takes up so much **SPACE.**

One of Ian's jokes:
Doctor, Doctor — I think I need glasses.
You certainly do, sir! This is a fish
and chip shop!

21.50 I've got another SPOT!
I might have to wear a paper bag over my head at school.

Wednesday, 25th August
8.20. Asked Mum again about having a baby guinea pig. She snapped, *Not now, Finch!* Also,

if she hears the words *guinea* and *pig* one more time she will SCREAM.

OK – so she was sitting on the loo. BUT I NEED TO KNOW! Had to remind her to leave some money to buy stuff for G's party. OK. I will not say another word! Will just wear my special pleading face.

17.45. Cassie came round today to help with the party grub. Got crisps, drinks and pizza. Made some crispie cakes and chocolate slices. But they were so scrummy that we ate most of them and had to make some more.

18.10 Made a poster with a picture of Graeme and a big speech bubble saying **PLEASE CAN I HAVE A GUINEA PIG HUTCH-BUDDY FOR MY BIRTHDAY? PLEASE! PLEASE! PLEASE! I BEG YOU!** Stuck it on the fridge door.

18.50. Mum says that she's still thinking about it. I bet she isn't. I bet she hasn't given it a millisecond's think. All she thinks about is Ian. I know exactly which one I want. I want the itsy-witsy baby girl guinea piggy-wiggy, with the most beautiful golden fur that grows in these little swirls and these big shiny pleading eyes saying, *Please Finch,* *be my mummy! Please Graeme, let me be your friend!*

19.50. ʙɪɢ BIG NEWS!

Ian is going to MOVE IN AND LIVE WITH US! I knew something was up from the way they kept eye-signalling each other. They made out they were asking me about it.

MUM: *We want to know how you feel about Ian moving in, love. (Soppy smile at Ian.)*

IAN: *It seems daft not to, really. But we want you to be happy about it. (Creepy smile at me.)*

MUM: *When Nolly comes home, it'll be much easier for all of us with him here.*

IAN: *Nolly thinks it's a good idea too.*
So I'm the last to know.

MUM: *She's thrilled about it. So, what d'you say, then, Finch? We'd really like to give it a proper go.*

So I said, *Do what you like.* I mean, he practically lives here anyway. I'll be perfectly OK, thanks a lot, all on my own and out of the way in my room downstairs.

20.15. I feel all mixed up. I want Mum to be happy but I want things to stay the same too. Just me, Mum and Nolly.
WORRY 6 Ian's moving into OUR house!

Nothing will ever be the same again. He's going to be here **ALL THE TIME!**
WORRY 7 What if it doesn't work out?
WORRY 8 What if Mum gets hurt?
WORRY 9 What if — loads of stuff.

20.10. GUESS WHAT! GUESS WHAT! Mum and Ian just called me out to the garden — and there was a little hutch! And inside the little hutch was a little baby guinea piggy! Jay told them which one I wanted. She is so **SCRUMPTIOUS!** She has these beautiful twinkly eyes — so I'm going to call her Twinkle. Graeme had a little sniff of her through the wire and was very excited. But Twinkle's a bit shy at the moment. We've put their hutches close together so they can get used to each other's smells and see each other.

Mum says Ian's bought the hutch and everything. But only 'cos he's trying to soften me up about him moving in. It's not that I hate him like I used to. But I just don't want his big hairy sprawly body here all the time. How am I going to survive????

Thursday, 26th August
GRAEME'S FOURTH BIRTHDAY!
21.25. Got tummy ache. Think I ate too much of Graeme's birthday cake. He LOVED the

treasure hunt we made for him. Jay brought some bits of plastic drainpipes and we hid little treats inside, like dandelions and apple chunks and bits of rusk. Twinkle's really getting used to me now. She pokes her nose out when I call her and she was out more in her run today. Graeme keeps trying to sniff her through the wire and she squeaks at him!

NEWSFLASH! NEWSFLASH! NEWSFLASH!

21.55. I'VE STARTED!

My periods have started! I can't believe it. Mum was snuggled up with Ian on the settee, so I stuck my head round the door, sending EMERGENCY eye-signals and muttering, *Mum – can you come here a minute?*

She just yawned. *What is it now, Finch? I'm too tired to move.*

It was ages till she got the message. I was signalling like some crazy loon that it was urgent! She's given me some pads – which took her for ever to find because she couldn't remember where she'd put them. She's dead chuffed now. So am I. I am a woman! Phoned Cassie with the news. Her's started ages ago. She gave me lots of gory details of her's. Ugh.

Friday, 27th August

8.45. Do I look different? Did some posing wearing my panty pads in front of the mirror. I definitely look more mature.

10.00. Did ten minutes' stroking and brushing Twinkle, then Graeme, so they got used to each other's smells from my hands and the brush. Graeme was sniffing like crazy and getting very excited. Have left him in his run next to Twinkle's, where they can see each other. Twinkle keeps running up to him, squeaking and sniffing through the wire, then running away. She's so funny!

15.05. Went round to Cassie's. She said, *You do realise that we could both have* **BABIES** *now?* I screamed, *No way!* She said, *I'm not saying I'm planning to! I'm only saying that it's POSSIBLE. Scary isn't it?*

18.15. Been shopping with Mum for new school uniform. Had a row over shoes. She thinks I'm still a little girl. Got a skirt and some trousers. The blazer's quite nice, but the sweatshirt is **GROSS!** Saw Leah. She'd just had her ears pierced.

I'm going to ask Mum if I can have my ears pierced.

18.35. She says NO! Wait till I'm a bit older! And why don't I use stick-ons. I'm twelve — not five! I mean, practically everyone I know has pierced ears. Joely Tranter has a pierced navel! Mum never used to be like this — all strict and fuddy-duddy. Quite the opposite. It's always been **ME** who's been the sensible one. I think Ian is too old for her. She's only twenty-nine. He's ancient — nearly **forty!**

21.15. Jay's got the nicest hands I've ever seen. When he was stroking Twinkle it made me go all goose-pimply! I'm going all goose-pimply now just thinking about it.

Saturday, 28th August

8.30. Got a card from Cassie with CONGRATULATIONS — YOU ARE A WOMAN NOW on it, and a collage made of tampons, pads with wings, and push-up bra ads with huge boobs that she'd cut out from magazine ads.

9.10. Ian here at the crack of dawn. Moving his stuff in already. Boxes and boxes of stuff.

10.05. It's so weird. When I went to the corner shop to get some milk, I really did feel different. I wonder if anyone noticed?

10.20. Cass phoned. Going to meet her at the mall at 12.30, then go back to her's.

10.35. YES! YES! YES! Can't believe it! Jay just phoned. He asked if I wanted to go to the pictures this afternoon! Just the **TWO** of us! So I sighed and said, *Mmmm – yeah, OK then,* very calmly as if I wasn't that bothered and as if I had loads more interesting things to do. But my heart was going **BOOM-BOOM-BOOM!** I'm meeting him at one o'clock. What am I going to wear? **What am I going to wear?????** What about Cass?

10.55. Phoned Cassie and said, Guess what! Jay and me are going to the pictures. Cass said, *Oh brill! I'll have his mate Dan then. What time?* Had to explain that it was just Jay and me. There was this long silence so I said, *Sorry Cass – oh, and thanks for the card. It made me laugh loads.* She said, *But you promised you were going to help me choose a top.* I said, *Yeah, I know. But that can wait, can't it? How about Monday instead?* She sighed, *Don't bother – I'll manage.*

11.10. I've got nothing to wear. Everything looks horrible! What about my spot? It's gone all scabby.

11.30. I'm borrowing Mum's pink skirt. She's small and I'm taller than her – so it fits OK. I'll wear my black vest top with the sequins. Mum keeps bouncing about, squealing, *Your first date! Your first date! Ooooh! How exciting!* Ian was leaning against the sink with this stupid grin on his face. So **EMBARASSING**. *It's no big deal,* I told them. Then Ian said, *Here – treat yourselves to some cola and popcorn.* And he gave me a tenner!

11.55. Spent five minutes brushing my teeth just in case Jay kisses me.

17.45. It was BRILLIANT! Jay bought some chips and we ate them walking about. Then we went to the pictures. I think he was a bit nervous because he kept wiping his hands on his jeans. I thought maybe he was wiping the sweat off so he could hold my hand, but then he bought this ginormous bucket of popcorn that needed both his hands.

When we'd finished the popcorn, he put his arm round me! It was nice at first, but after a bit I got a crick in the neck. Then his hand crept on to mine – and I went all **tingle-tingly!** Afterwards we went to **The Ice Cream-Dream**

25

Machine and he bought me a *Tahiti Sweetie* – which was vanilla and mango ice cream, with coconut sauce, and bananas. He had *Pecan American* – which was nuts and chocolate sauce and maple ice cream. And halfway through he put a spoonful into my mouth – and I went all gooey! Then he did this enormous fake burp – and stuck a straw up each nostril. Then I came home. He didn't kiss me, though. Why not? What's wrong with me? It must have cost him loads. I offered to pay half but he wouldn't let me. Won't tell Ian – he might want his tenner back. Jay is SOOOOO COOL. Mmmmmm...

18.15. Cassie phoned.
She asked, *Did he kiss you, then?*
Yeah.
Where? How! Tell me!
I can't...
On the lips?
Maybe.
What was it like? Slobbery? Slurpy?
Cass...
Tell me! Tell me!
So what sort of top did you get then, Cass?

Mum and Ian were listening to EVERY word! There's no privacy in this house!

18.40. Just realised something gross! I knew —
but what with Jay and everything it went out
of my head — **IAN WILL BE STAYING THE
NIGHT HERE,** won't he!!! It'll be like their first
official night together — like a honeymoon!
They'll be upstairs — doing it! And I'll be
downstairs. **Cringe-cringe! Squirm-squirm!**

I don't want to be here! I've got to ring
Cassie and see if I can stay there!

Cass says it's a bit tricky. Her mum and dad
had a big row this morning. (But they're
always having arguments.) She's going to ring
me back.

18.50. Cass rang to say I can sleep over. But
only if I tell her EVERYTHING about Jay.

Sunday, 29th August

10.40. Back from Cassie's. Straightaway Mum
had a go at me because I forgot to feed
Graeme and Twinkle before I left! I feel
terrible, but I wouldn't have forgotten if it
hadn't been for Ian being here and everything!
I've given them extra strokes and cuddles to
make up for it. Told Cass that Jay didn't really
kiss me. She was really disappointed 'cos she'd
made up this **KISS QUIZ** for me to answer.
E.g. Were his lips soft or hard? Did you close
your eyes or leave them open? Did your noses
get in the way?

She's getting all anxious about starting at St Mon's and would do anything to come with me to Fletchley High. That's what her mum and dad's big row was about. Her dad backed her up, saying it's a waste of money if Cassie doesn't want to go.

15.00. The house doesn't seem like ours any more. Ian's things are everywhere. I cannot believe how much stuff he's got! Have tripped over his big smelly boots a million times. Have had to put up with his CDs belting out. Every now and then Mum and him start dancing round the furniture like totally mad people. Ian's computer will come in very useful though. Thank goodness I'm sharing Nolly's bathroom. At least I won't have to put up with PHEWY Ian-pongs!

WORRY 10 Why hasn't Jay phoned? Should I phone him? What if he's gone off me?

21.40. Visited Nolly in hospital. She says they're keeping her in against her will, and that if the heart-attack didn't kill her the hospital cooking will. She's dying to get her teeth into a decent steak and kidney pudding.

21.50. Was it that scabby spot on my nose that put Jay off me?

Monday, 30th August

9.10. I am all alone. Cassie's going to see this new friend of her's from St Monica's. Her name is Rachel. Cassie met her at *Henley's* where they were buying school uniforms and discovered she lives in the next road. She sounds a bit boring to me.

10.07 Rang Jay. No answer. Can you die of boredom?

11.15. Rearranged Nolly's Virgin Marys. Mum had shoved them both on to Nolly's sideboard like they were having a gossip. Nolly likes to have one Mary on her sideboard and the other one on her bedroom mantelpiece.

11.45. Made some little WELCOME HOME NOLLY! flags for the two Marys to wave for when Nolly comes home from hospital.

12.16. Had a peek in Mum and Ian's bedroom. It's very tidy — not like Mum's old room used to be. Ian is a right old housewife. Had a snoop. Nothing interesting. Thank goodness! Is it really only **13.57**?
It's now **13.59.** The phone will ring any minute...now!

14.00. Maybe it's like that horror film I saw – a deadly alien killer ray has killed the entire population and I'm the last person alive...

14.08. The phone's ringing...!

14.10. Wrong number.

14.37. Sharpened my pencils, packed my school bag.

14.50. I'm getting fed up with long hair. Shall I have it cut off?

15.10. Fetched Graeme in for cuddles. Took my socks off and let him nibble my toes. That always makes me laugh.

21.20 The most **BORING** day of my life.

Tuesday, 31st August

9.40. Put Graeme into Twinkle's run. His little nose was twitching like mad. Twinkle is still a bit shy. She keeps peeking out of her hutch – then hiding. After a bit she came out and they had a good sniff of each other. Then Graeme started honking his happy little **I Love You** noises that he makes when I stroke him. And now they're snuggled up in the corner together! Graeme has a little bump on his head. I think it's because he'd been bashing it against the wire to get through to Twinkle.

15.40. Been to Cassie's. Her school uniform is disgusting. They have to wear these YUCKY grey and maroon stripy blazers and maroon pleated shirts. She's right – they do make her look like Mrs Toad of Toad Hall. Her new friend Rachel came round. She's got this long pale face and straight blonde hair. All they talked about was St Monica's – so I came home. They don't start school till next week. It's HORRIBLE being at home on my own! I so miss having Nolly around.

15.55. I'm going to call Jay. Maybe he's been waiting for me to call – like I've been waiting for him.

15.59. His mum said he's out with Dan and won't be back till this evening. Yawn, yawn yawn!

16.15. NEWSFLASH! Mum called to say that Nolly will be coming home on Saturday!

16.50. Made a brilliant card for Nolly, with Mum and me, Graeme and Twinkle and the two Virgin Marys on it, waving their WELCOME HOME flags – one's holding a bottle of Scotch whisky for her. Just managed to squeeze in a very tiny Ian, as there wasn't much space left.

17.40. Graeme and Twinkle follow one another around all the time! They are so cute!

18.10. J STILL HASN'T CALLED. What's the matter? Have I got smelly breath or something?

18.20. Mum says I haven't got smelly breath. Then she said, *Maybe he's a bit nervous about phoning you. You didn't scare him off did you?* I said, *Uh? What d'you mean?* And she said, *Well, you can be a little bossy sometimes.* I AM **NOT** BOSSY!

First day at Fletchley High tomorrow!
Phoned Kayleigh. We're going to meet with Carmen by the post office and we'll walk together to school. We've decided to wear skirts, not trousers.

18.45. My hair-drier's broken. Gave it to Ian to mend. Also my clock radio. Told him my window is stuck too. And my bike chain needs fixing.

19.30. Jay turned up with Dan! (To see how Twinkle was getting on with Graeme, he said.)

Mum let him in without a
word. I was watching telly
with a green lime and
cucumber face mask on and
my hair all wet and straggly!
Dan said, *Where do you keep
your broomstick, then?* And
they both cracked up. I'm going
to wipe it from my memory banks. I've
noticed that Jay is not so mature when he's
with Dan.

21.15. Mum just had a go at me for
monopolising the phone for nearly two hours.
Monopolising? Where did she get that from?
Ian, that's where! Anyway, it was an
emergency! Had to tell Cassie about J and the
embarrassing face mask. Cassie is bored
because St Monica's doesn't start for another
two weeks. Also she's panicking that no one
will like her. Told her we will ALWAYS be
friends.
    I think I'll wear plaits tomorrow.

21.30. Complained to Mum about people who
monopolise the settee ALL EVENING. Ha ha ha.

Wednesday, 1st September
First day at Fletchley High.
17.40. Feel really fed up.
1. Kayleigh lied. They both wore trousers! Only

two of us wore skirts! Me and a
girl with fat legs called Donna.
2. In history Kayleigh and
Carmen sat with two other
girls – and there was no room
for me!
3. They didn't wait for me
at break time. I hate them.
4. Jay was playing football every break time
and ignored me...
5. Everyone kept tugging my plaits.
**6. Everyone except me has a friend! No
one likes me!**

Called at Cassie's on the way home to tell
her about my horrible day but boring Rachel
was there again. She had the nerve to glare at
me like I was interrupting something private.
They'd been prancing around to some music in
the sitting room – I saw them through the
window as I walked up the path. I only stayed
for about five minutes. Don't know what Cass
sees in Rachel.

19.15. Cass phoned and asked if I was ⊙K. She
said I looked dead miz when I called round.
She's getting worked up about starting school
next week. Said I thought that Rachel was
boring. Cass said, *Yeah, I know, but I don't
have any choice – she's the only friend I'll
have when I start at St Monica's.* Told her

about MY HORRIBLE DAY. She says she never liked Kayleigh anyway – she's two-faced. Thank goodness I have Graeme. He can always tell when I'm upset. I'm keeping him in my room tonight. He's snuggled up beside me. I'll wear trousers and a ponytail tomorrow.

Thursday, 2nd September

16.20. All day long Kayleigh and Carmen kept staring at me, whispering and sniggering. Who wants to be friends with them anyway!

Had games today – and showers! I felt SO nervous. It's stupid really because Mum and me never shut the bathroom door or anything. But I acted like it didn't bother me. And I tried to sneak a peek at everyone else without seeming like a pervert or something. I've never seen so many girls with their kit off! Some are TOTALLY FLAT! Some have HUGE boobs. Most are in between. A couple of girls were really hairy! And some had none at all. I think I'm quite normal. Phew.

Feel a bit better today 'cos I made friends with the girl with fat legs who I sat next to in English. Her name is Donna Siddley. She has the most perfect nose I have ever seen, but very bushy eyebrows. She's coming round after school tomorrow.

21.00. Graeme has the cleverest new trick! He keeps jumping over Twinkle. We were all in hysterics — even Ian! Graeme's eye keeps watering, though — it looks like he's crying. Ian had a look but couldn't find anything wrong. Twinkle squeaked with excitement when we put Graeme back in the run. They look so sweet cuddled up together, but I'm keeping Graeme in my room tonight. He's cuddled up next to me in bed. Forgot to clean the hutches out! Too late now.

Friday, 3rd September

19.20. Donna came round after school. She started going through all my drawers and cupboards! *Oh my God — aren't you tidy? How* WEIRD! she said. Then she started on my dressing table, trying on my chocolate-mint lipgloss and blusher without even asking. She was so nosey! She had the cheek to tell me to stick to trousers, as my legs are too thin for skirts! She said, *You must disguise your flaws and emphasise your best features, which is why skirts are good for me because I have very good legs.* NOT! Her legs are like tree trunks.
NOLLY COMES HOME TOMORROW! YIPPEE!

Saturday, 4th September

10.15. Don't feel like writing. Can't stop crying. Graeme has DIED! Twinkle came running out when I went to feed them this morning, but not Graeme. I found him all curled up and cold in his hutch bedroom. My eyes are little red slits from crying. Even when I write it down I can't believe it. Everything's going wrong. I **HATE** school. I hate it! Cass and me have been split up – and now Graeme's DIED! And it's probably all MY fault! I'm sorry Graeme! I'm so sorry. Why didn't I get Mum to take you to the vet? It was that bump and your watery eye. I know it was! Twinkle keeps squeaking and looking for him. I've brought her indoors to keep me company. Phoned to tell Cass but her mum says she's staying at Rachel's. Asked her to tell Cass it was REALLY, REALLY URGENT. I need you, Cass!

12.20. Nolly's home. She likes her new flat. I still can't stop crying about Graeme though. I had him from when I was eight. That's a **THIRD** of my life!

Sunday, 5th September

13.30. Nolly's got loads of pills to take. She says she might be tempted to go back into hospital if I don't stop wailing on about Graeme and that I've got a bad case of the Green Meanies — which she knows a lot about because they squirmed their way inside her head when she was in hospital. She says they kept whispering stuff like, *You've had it, lass. Your ticker's all in. Silly old bat! You wouldna listen when Finch nagged you to give up the ciggies.* She says the Meanies like to bring you down and get you feeling sorry for yourself. If you let them, they take over, growing fatter and fatter, till there's no room for nice thoughts, only miz ones. The way to get rid of them is to think about the happy times, like when Graeme accidentally got shut in the airing cupboard and chewed up my favourite pink jumper to make a nest. When we found him he looked like a bright pink rabbit! And how he used to make happy grunts when I stroked him, and the way he'd dash about, leaping and hopping when he was let out on the grass. BOO-HOO. It just makes me cry more. But the Green Meanies can get lost because now I know it wasn't my fault that Graeme died. Ian phoned the vet yesterday and she said that Graeme's bump was probably an abscess, which was pressing on his eye — that's why it was watering. She said lots of rabbits get them — and he wasn't in pain or anything. And even if we'd taken him to her there was not much she could have done. So there, Green Meanies! You can get lost! It wasn't my fault! ZAP! ZAP! But I'm going to miss you so much, Graeme.

14.20. Cass phoned. She's coming round.

20.30. Cass and me gave Graeme a good funeral. We put him in a shoebox with his favourite nibbles and buried him under the apple tree. Then we chanted, *Happy journey Graeme, to the great warren in the sky. We wish you a bunny paradise of everlasting Cheerios and fields of soft green grass and lots of juicy grapes. May you hop happily in bunny heaven for ever and ever.* Then I started blubbing again. It's really spooky that I had that dream about Graeme growing wings. Maybe I'm psychic.

Green Meanie Thought 1. It's school tomorrow. Meanie-zapper 1. I'm not worried that I haven't made a proper friend yet. I'm picky — I don't want just anyone. Especially Nosey Donna. I'm going to act cool and mysterious. ZAP!
Green Meanie Thought 2. I'll have to go around with that boring girl called Kerry

Jones that I was paired up with in maths on Friday. She's got great hair though, thick black dead straight hair, really shiny and down to just below her shoulders, and it swishes when she moves, like that shampoo ad...

Meanie-zapper 2. But only until I become so popular that I have the pick of some more interesting friends. ZAP!

I keep thinking that Graeme is still here, snuffling about my room. Then I remember. Maybe he's a ghost bunny!!! You can come and haunt me if you like Graeme. I'd love a ghost bunny. Please haunt me!

Mum's taking next week off work to help Nolly settle in. I wish I could take a week off school.

Monday, 6th September

18.45. I only managed cool and mysterious till lunchtime. It was more like I was invisible. Went round with Kerry. She did this dead funny impression of Mrs Smedley in C.D.T who keeps heaving her bosoms up and hisses all her s's. E.g. Brian Palmer, you may see yourss-self as the class-ss comedian — but I find you tedious-ssly unfunny. And then she gives this killer smile. Brian Palmer had been making farting noises on his arm. Also he keeps sneaking up on girls and pinching them on the bum. He'd better not try it on me. Jay played football at every break. He did wave at me though.

Dropped in on Cassie on the way home. (Rachel not there – FOR A CHANGE!) Cass had a notice stuck to her bedroom door saying: YES, MUM, I DO HAVE TO SLOUCH. NO, MUM, I CAN'T DO ANYTHING WITH MY HAIR 'COS I LIKE IT LIKE THIS.

She put it there to stop her mum asking her the same two questions a million times a day. She says she's so bored and fed up that she's almost looking forward to starting at St Monica's.

Mum says she's exhausted trying to stop Nolly bustling about. She found her cleaning the windows this morning. We both had a go at her.

19.30. Twinkle squeaks every time she sees me now and stands up with her little paws on the hutch wire, waiting for me to pick her up. She still keeps looking for Graeme though.

Tuesday, 7th September
16.50. We had something called P.S.H.E today, which stands for Personal, Social and Health Education. Miss Moody took us for it. She wasn't a bit moody – she was really nice – and wore this fantastic suede skirt and red

high-heeled boots. She told us that it was perfectly normal if any of us were feeling a bit lost or nervous in our new school and said that if we had any worries or problems we should tell our form tutor or her. Then she asked if anyone had a worry or problem they'd like to discuss. Not one hand went up. And no way was I going to put up my hand and say, *Yes, Miss, my problem is I don't have a single real friend at this school.* Then she passed some paper round and told us to write down any worries and problems that kids might have, anything at all – no matter how silly or embarrassing – but not to put our names on the papers. Soon, everyone was scribbling like mad. I wrote MAKING FRIENDS. She collected all the papers in a box, which she shoved under her desk, then told us to get our rough books out. There was this huge roar of kids complaining, *Aren't you going to read them out, Miss?* Miss Moody smiled and said, *But I thought you weren't that interested. Are you sure you want to know?* And everyone was nodding, *YEAH! We do! We do! Read them out!*

So she did. The first one said: HAVING SMELLY FEET. And everyone laughed. Then there was, PARENTS WHO ARGUE ALL THE TIME, DRUGS, MAKING FRIENDS, (loads of those), MY MUM'S ILL, SPOTS, WAR, VERRUCAS, I HATE P.E, HAVING THE RIGHT CLOTHES, THE ENVIRONMENT, I HATE MY STEPSISTER, BULLIES, SEX, BEING TOO SKINNY, BEING FAT, WANTING PEOPLE TO LIKE YOU...a whole box of worries. And we all sat there in total silence wondering who had written what.

Miss Moody told us that the worries we'd written down were the same sort of worries that other classes had listed, but sometimes kids didn't know where to go for help. The school had been awarded some extra money last term and it was decided to use it to set up a scheme to help kids with worries or problems. They'd run a school competition to come up with ideas — and lots of interesting suggestions had come in — but there was still time to enter if any of us had ideas. The deadline is Friday 17th September. And then the bell went. And everyone went, *Aaaaw!* Because we'd all got really interested.

17.20. Just thought, it's time for a cuddle with Graeme. Then I remembered. Waaaaah! I'm all mopey now.

18.45. Searched the flat for photos of Graeme — found five. Stuck them on my wardrobe. *Hello Graeme!*

21.40. *Night-night Graeme!* ✗ ✗ ✗ ✗

Wednesday, 8th September

16.45. Mr Morris took us for art today.
There were six of us on a big table — Jay,
Dan and another boy with a long nose, called
Trevor, a girl called Narinder and her friend
Mia who has this amazing reddish-golden
wavy hair, just like Rapunzel, though not long
enough for a prince to climb up, just down to
her waist, and tied back, and me. Kerry was
forced to sit at another table 'cos just as she
was about to sit down, the rude and annoying
Trevor grabbed her chair. But when
Kerry tried to grab it back Mr
Morris barked at her to stop fussing!
Then we had to do drawings of our
shoes. Then Trevor started sneering
at my drawing, saying it looked more
like an armoured tank than a shoe and he
scribbled these guns firing explosions on it
and everyone laughed. Worse still, Jay started
telling Rapunzel that her drawing was
brilliant, and how did she learn to draw so
well etc.

Suddenly my eyes went all watery — and
these embarrassing tears started running down
my face. I felt a total airhead 'cos I'm not a
dopey crybaby sort. Narinder noticed and
nudged Mia, so I said, *Ooops, sorry about
that. It's just that my rabbit Graeme died.*

Trevor thought this was funny and started snorting with laughter. Rapunzel told him, *It's not funny.* But she was smiling. Trevor said it was because Graeme was a weird name for a rabbit. Then Narinder said, *You could always get another one.* Like Graeme could be replaced like a toothbrush or something! I said *What!* And Rapunzel sighed, *It's not exactly the end of the world, is it?* So I said, *YES IT IS! FOR GRAEME IT IS! Anyway, how would you know!* She rolled her eyes at Narinder like I was truly sad and Narinder glared daggers at me. Jay sort of glanced up at me but he didn't back me up or anything. I think he likes arty-farty Rapunzel now! How would she like it if one of her best friends died? I feel dead depressed. She and Narinder kept looking at me and whispering together all through art.

21.15. Mum goes back to work tomorrow. We've all told Nolly she's got to take things easy today. Mum's organised for her to have her dinner delivered by *Meals on Wheels.* Also she's got one of those alarm buttons that old people can wear round their necks. If she falls over or feels ill or something, all she has to do is press it and call for help.

21.50. My drawing was **MUCH** better than Rapunzel's! Before Trevor scribbled all over it! Why didn't Jay say something about mine? Eh? Why? Why? Why? I am VERY upset. Tried phoning Cass for a good moan but keep getting the answerphone.

Thursday, 9th September

16.50. **Embarrassing or what?** Ian met me outside school in his van, with **HANDYMAN TANNER – THE MAN WITH THE SPANNER! REPAIRS, PAINTING AND DECORATING, DRAINS AND GUTTERS CLEARED** all over it. He honked the horn, leaned out and yelled, *Oi! Finch! Wanna lift?*

Is that your boyfriend? asked some stupid boy. **PERLEEEESE!**

Nolly was weeding the garden when we got home! And she wasn't wearing her alarm button! She says the *Meals on Wheels* didn't turn up till 2.30 and it was so disgusting that she's told them not to bother again – she'll cook her own dinner thank you very much. Mum gave her a ticking off but Nolly said, *Listen lass, I may have had a wee heart attack, but I've not lost the use of my brain or my limbs, and I won't be mollycoddled!* She had better not start smoking again. I will have to watch her very carefully.

Newsflash! Think Jay does still fancy me! He and Dan shared our table at lunchtime –

it was too wet for football. Jay gave me half his Snickers bar! And said my hair looked cool in bunches!

Friday, 10th September

17.50. Ian's been here a week too long already! He thinks he is SO funny. *Is that phone surgically attached to your ear?* he asked when I was on the phone to Cassie.

Ha ha ha, but excuse me, I said, *this is OUR phone, not yours.*

Excuse ME, he sighed, *it's your mum's phone. And it's her and me who'll be paying the bills. Can't it wait till cheap rate after six?*

It was urgent! I had loads to tell Cassie about how Rapunzel and Narinder were being total pains at school again. When Kerry and me went to the loos, they were both there in front of the mirrors. Narinder was doing Rapunzel's hair and Rapunzel was admiring herself from all angles with this little hand mirror. She rolled her eyes at Narinder and groaned, *Oh no — look who's here.* As we tried to get past, we got facefuls of styling spritzer. Kerry said, *Oh, thanks a lot! That went in my eye! I can't blink now!* Narinder rolled her eyes at Rapunzel and sighed, *Just ignore them. They're not worth it.* So I said, *Look — what IS your problem!* Narinder glared and said, *What's YOUR problem, BIRD-BRAIN!*

So I snapped, *Do NOT call me Bird-brain!* And Rapunzel huffed, *Don't get your feathers in a twist, Bird-brain! We're leaving!* And they flounced off. Kerry called, *BETTER TO BE A BIRD-BRAIN THAN AN AIRHEAD!* And I called, *OR A HAIRHEAD!* We were laughing so much that we had to lean against the wall. Which is weird 'cos it wasn't that funny, but we were in a mad sort of mood. Cass was very quiet on the phone. I said, *Are you still there, Cass?* She sighed, *Yeah. I think so. It's just that I'm so bored, I'm not sure.*

Saturday, 11th September

10.40. Mum and Ian have taken Nolly out for the day. They won't be back till teatime. The flat is mine! All mine! Hee-hee-hee. Cass, Kerry, Jay and Dan are on their way. Little Twinkle keeps trying to eat my cereal!

21.30. Had a really great day. Watched a video then we made some crispie cakes. Gave everyone a guided tour of Graeme's grave, and left a crispie cake for him on top. We got talking about our pets. Kerry told us about a pet worm she had when she was little. His name was Sidney and one day she put him on the window ledge so he could see the garden — but she forgot all about him and he got shrivelled up by the sun. She says she cried for days and still feels bad about it. Then we played *Twister*, which made Cass laugh so uncontrollably that she dribbled chewed-up crispie cake all over the back of Dan's T-shirt. We didn't hear Mum, Nolly and Ian arrive home — until Ian barged in with, *Aha! So this is where all the cups and mugs have disappeared to. Might we bother you for a couple, please? And could this be someone's toast and jam left by the phone? Oh, I see you managed to finish off the chocolate digestives then?* So I said, *Yes thanks. It was quite a challenge, but we did it.* Then Mum started on about a few teeny-weeny guinea pig poos on the settee and the carpet. So what's the vacuum cleaner for, then?

Sunday, 12th September

Mum and Ian are being cringe-makingly dopey-smoochy-giggly today. And now Nolly's got her Tom Jones's records belting out next door. She says she feels twenty years younger since her heart attack, which makes her fifty-three now. Can't hear myself think. I'm off to Cassie's.

17.40. Cass was still in bed when I got there. She said she was too depressed to get up. So I got in with her and we decided to do a mammoth whingeing lie-in about THINGS I HATE ABOUT MY LIFE. Cassie's list was, being forced to go to St Monica's, being nagged about her hair, the clothes she wears, and the clothes that she refuses to wear. Getting the blame for causing arguments between her mum and dad (about not wanting to go to St Monica's), being ungrateful (about St Mon's), also for refusing to wear this yucky dress her mum bought her yesterday, lying in bed, slouching, sighing, slamming doors, etc, etc. She said, *It's like she wants me to be* **THE PERFECT DAUGHTER** *or something.* Then I had this idea – for her to pretend to be like that and see what happened. So we flattened all her hair and gripped it back with hair clips, and she put on the yucky dress and then she went downstairs and pranced into the sitting room where her mum and dad were reading the papers, fluttering her eyelashes and twittering, *What do you think, Mumsy-wumsy? Do I look pretty now? Please say I do! Oh, and let me get you both a nice cup of tea, Mummy and Daddy darlings.* Her dad laughed and her mum sighed, *Oh yes, very amusing, Cassandra.* But she couldn't help smiling a little bit.

Monday, 13th September
16.20. Phoned Cass to see how she got on at St Monica's. No one there. Left a message.

Had music today with Mr Curtis. He's really young and so good-looking. Kerry was swooning about him. After, as we were walking along the corridor to maths, Kerry said, *Hey, look at this.* It was a newspaper cutting pinned to a noticeboard, showing a photo of a sponsored walk by teachers and kids, all waving at the camera — all except for Mr Curtis, who was giving a piggy-back to some small kid. Kerry got out her pen and gave Mrs Enderby a speech balloon and wrote inside it, *HANDS UP AND WAVE EVERYONE WHO THINKS MR CURTIS IS CUTE AND SEXY. Ho ho ho!*

No Rapunzel today. Narinder kept giving me black looks though.

18.10. Cass phoned. She says St Mon's was OK and she's made millions of friends (three actually), all new girls, plus Rachel. She sounded quite cheerful. I feel sort of jealous.

Tuesday, 14th September
16.10. P.S.H.E was EXCELLENT today. Miss Moody brought in this pile of teen mags and read some of the questions out, like, *My friends have started shoplifting and say I can't be friends if I don't join in. What shall I do?* We had to work in fours and come up with answers

— some of them were really good.

My answer was, *That's blackmail! What kind of friends would do that to you? Get some new friends.*

Jay said, *You wouldn't be asking this question if you knew it was OK to join in.* Kerry's was, *Don't even think about it! You have a brain, don't you? Use it!*

Dan's was, *Just remember, you could get caught.*

P.S.H.E is definitely my favourite lesson and Miss Moody is my favourite teacher. I'd love to be an agony aunt on a mag!

17.45. Jay called round to show me his new bike! Nolly made us banana milkshakes. Then Jay noticed Ian's computer so he showed me how I could send him emails, so I wrote, *Hi, Jay! This is Finch. Tweet-tweet! Write back. See ya! Byeee!* We're all going round later to see his computer.

20.20. Just got back from Jay's. We found some amazing websites for kids — even one on rabbits! Then Kerry started reading out letters on the problem page from her magazine and we began making up silly answers. Suddenly I had this BRILLIANT IDEA! The others think it's brilliant too. The trouble is we haven't got much time.

20.50. Ian wanted to know who'd been using his computer. He knew someone had because their crisp crumbs were on it, and do I know what sort of damage that could cause? Also there was a message for **ME**! It was from Jay and said, *What d'you make the answer to number four, maths homework?* And there were all these pink and blue hopping rabbits all over it!

21.15. Ian says that I can use the computer! *But only on condition you don't mess up my files or bring any food or drink anywhere near it, and remember, like the phone, email costs MONEY! So don't go mad,* blah blah blah. He's even set up my very own email address and folder – with a secret password number so that only I can open it! He's ⊙K. Sometimes.

Wednesday, 15th September
7.30. THE BRILLIANT IDEA is...a school website for YEAR EIGHT children with worries and problems! I couldn't get to sleep for thinking about it. All that kids have to do is email their problems to the website, then other kids can email their ideas in! We haven't decided on a name for it yet. We've only got till Friday to get it to Miss Moody

for the competition, so we're meeting round at Jay's again after school tomorrow. The names we've come up with so far are:

WHAT'S YOUR PROBLEM?
WHAT'S YOUR WORRY?
WORRY WARTS
WHAT'S BUGGING YOU?
HELP!

Thursday, 16th September

8.00. Feel really tired because I got woken up in the middle of the night by Nolly's phone ringing. It only rang twice but I couldn't get back to sleep for ages. Who would ring Nolly at that time of night? She says she didn't hear it. *That's probably because you make so much noise talking in your sleep,* I told her. I could hear her though the wall. She was mumbling and chuckling away to herself for ages.

19.45. We finished our website plan. We've decided to call it **WHAT'S YOUR PROBLEM?** We've got some great ideas for graphics called **WORRY BUGS.** They're like little creepy-crawly monsters – spotty bugs for people with spots, and monster-scary bugs for different fears and phobias, nasty bully bugs, and all kinds of wriggly-squirmy worry bugs, with speech balloons, muttering stuff like, *No one likes*

you! and *I'm gonna get you!* We planned it all
out and made a special folder for it.
It looks great, with drawings of kids
with different expressions — tearful,
puzzled, spotty, lonely, or with
stinky feet — all being tortured by
the worry bugs. We're going to give
it to Miss Moody tomorrow. This is our
design for the website welcome page.

WELCOME TO
WHAT'S YOUR PROBLEM?

Fletchley High School's
very own website for

WORRY WARTS

Designed by YEAR EIGHT KIDS for

YOU

SO, IF YOU HAVE A PROBLEM
or think YOU CAN HELP
email us at
WYP?@fletchleyhigh.gov.uk
Or click here
WYP?@fletchleyhigh.gov.uk
Don't let the WORRY BUGS get you!
But remember...

EVERYTHING MUST BE
STRICTLY CONFIDENTIAL

Do not use your full name — only use your first
name or a code name

WISH 12 I wish that our WHAT'S YOUR PROBLEM? website idea wins!

Friday, 17th September
16.15. We gave the folder to Miss Moody first thing. She said she looked forward to reading it!

Saturday, 18th September
11.00 Cass came round. I knew something was wrong straight away so I asked her if it was about school. She said, *No. It's my mum and dad. They're going to get a divorce.* She knows that they haven't been getting on for ages but it's still a big shock. They've just decided that it will be best for everyone and her dad is going to move out into a flat. She says that her little brother Leo is really upset about it and keeps saying, *Don't go Daddy! Please don't go!*

I feel really sorry for them, even for Leo who is a pain most of the time. Cass is truly distraught. She gets on better with her dad than with her mum usually – he sticks up for her. I told her about Nolly's Green Meanies – and zapping them with nice thoughts, like at least she won't have to put up with her mum and dad rowing any more. She screamed, *What stupid rubbish! I haven't got any happy thoughts! It's my mum and dad I'd like to zap right now!* She calmed down a bit after Nolly came in and gave her a cuddle. Then she went home because she was worried about Leo.

Sunday, 19th September

10.15. A really **WEIRD** thing. I found Mum in the kitchen scoffing ice cubes from the fridge. She says she just felt like it 'cos they're nice and cold and crunchy and refreshing. Yeah, right, Mum.

10.40. Phoned Cass. Her mum said she'd gone to stay at Rachel's. Why didn't she ask to come and stay here? *I'm* her best friend, not Rachel.

15.45. A really, really, really **AMAZING THING!** Jay phoned and said, *Remember when you came round at the beginning of the holidays to see my baby guinea pigs?*
  So I said, *Yeah, of course I do.*
  And do you remember that I was looking after Dan's rabbit, Pepsi?
  Yeah. 'Cos Dan was on holiday.
  Right — and do you remember that you brought Graeme to help you choose one of the babies as a hutch bunny for him? And how later we found Graeme got inside Pepsi's run?
  Yeah.

Well, Graeme was a very busy little bunny because Dan told me that Pepsi's just given birth to four baby bunnies. You get what I'm saying?

I was jumping up and down with excitement, screaming, *Graeme is a daddy!* I wanted to rush round and see the babies but you're not supposed to disturb them when they're just born. If human smells get on to the babies the mother rabbit might eat them! I've got to wait **TEN WHOLE DAYS** before it's safe to handle them. I want a baby bunny! I want a baby bunny! I MUST have one of Graeme's babies!

16.00. Had to interrupt an embarrassing **SMOOCHING** session between Mum and Ian to beg on my knees for one of Graeme's babies. They looked at one another, and then Mum nodded. *Why not? The more the merrier!* Then they collapsed into crazy laughter. They laugh at the weirdest things. They've been totally dopey all weekend.

16.15. I still can't believe it! **GRAEME IS A DADDY!** Graeme lives on in his babies!

16.40. Phoned Cass to tell her. No answer. Answerphone not switched on either. It's her birthday next Wednesday. I wonder if Cassie would like a bunny for her birthday. That might cheer her up. She could keep it in the

special pet house they have at St Monica's.
I wish we had a pet house at my school.

Monday, 20th September

16.15. Rapunzel was back today,
unfortunately. We were coming out of music
when Narinder glared at me and snorted, *Who
are you staring at!* I said, *What?* I hadn't a
clue what she was talking about. Then
Rapunzel snorted, *Don't waste time on them!
They're not worth it!* As they stomped off,
Kerry called after them, *Keep your hair on!*
Which cracked us up because Rapunzel had
her hair in this new piled-up style, like she
thinks she's a model or something. Passed Miss
Moody in the corridor but she didn't say
anything about our WHAT'S YOUR PROBLEM?
website. Can't stop drawing baby bunnies.
They're hopping all over my rough book.

16.40. Phoned Cassie again.
Just the answerphone. Left
a message to ring me.

19.20. Caught Mum
crunching ice cubes again!

20.45. Have tried phoning Cass
loads of times. It's like they've gone
away or something. Hope she's OK.

Tuesday, 21st September

P.S.H.E today! I bet Miss Moody is stunned by our brilliant website idea. Can't wait to see the look on everyone's faces when she raves about it! Especially Rapunzel and Narinder's faces. Ha ha ha!

16.20. Miss Moody made not one itsy-witsy mention of our WHAT'S YOUR PROBLEM? folder! The whole lesson was spent filling in questionnaires about bullying! We stayed behind and asked her about it. She said she didn't have time to talk about it now. But she had time for Rapunzel and Narinder who were hanging about waiting to see her too and kept looking at Kerry and me like we were deadly enemies. She shooed us out, called R and N in, and closed the door.

Wednesday, 22nd September

Cassie's thirteenth birthday.

8.05. Tried phoning Cassie again, but still no one there. Where is she? Keep yawning. Nolly was mumbling in her sleep again and laughing. I tried counting rabbits – then had this really weird dream of Graeme on a giant cloud that was raining all these baby bunnies down to earth.

16.30. Had a HORRENDOUS day. During art

there was a message for Kerry, me, Narinder and Mia Rapunzel-head to go and see Miss Moody. At first we thought it must be about our website plan, but it seemed strange that she didn't send for Jay and Dan too.

When we got there, Miss Moody said to Kerry and me, *We need to talk about a serious matter. Narinder feels that you have some sort of hate campaign against Mia.* We were totally **STUNNED!**

What? said Kerry. *We haven't done anything!* Narinder accused us of staring at and making fun of Mia! We said that it was more like the other way round! We were only sticking up for ourselves. Then Mia said, *They keep following us to the loos!* We said, *We didn't follow them – we didn't even know they were there!* Miss Moody said, *Well, perhaps there's been some misunderstanding.* But the look on her face said, *Oh, poor pretty Mia-rella – being bullied by the two ugly sisters!* She made us apologise! It was so humiliating. We even had to shake hands with them. Then she let them go but kept **US** back, and told us that she hoped there wouldn't be any more trouble and that we must be more considerate to other people's feelings because Mia was going through a difficult patch at the moment. It was so unfair! We were there for ages and missed all of art! We are going to totally ignore them both from now on. Mia was excused games for some dopey reason. She acts like a princess.

17.00. Still no Cassie. I'm dying to tell her about horrible Rapunzel and Narinder.

WORRY 11 Where is Cass? I hope she's all right.

18.45. Cassie phoned. She's just got back. Her mum has been a bit depressed so they all went to stay at Cassie's grandparents. Went round to give her my birthday present, which was a gift voucher I designed:

> To be exchanged for One Baby Bunny, plus accessories: hay, straw, feeding bottle and pellets.

She said it would be cruelty to animals to make a bunny live with her family at this moment in time. Her dad has moved out, her mum's all weepy, and Leo's being a pain. It was the worst birthday of her life and she really misses her dad. She's upset about being taken out of school to visit her grandparents just as she was beginning to settle in. I'll have to think of another present for her.

Thursday, 23rd September

At lunchtime Miss Moody told me, Kerry, Jay and Dan that the WHAT'S YOUR PROBLEM?

website idea didn't win. This was because some of the teachers had concerns about it. Then she reeled off this long list.

1. It would need expensive computer equipment.
2. It would get in the way of schoolwork.
3. Some kids would use it to waste time and send stupid messages.
4. It would need at least one volunteer teacher to monitor it and teachers are already overworked and don't have the time.
5. It would need a room or office in school to operate from... I forget the other reasons.

The winning idea was from Year Ten for Bullying Awareness and Counselling – which will be announced in Whole School Assembly tomorrow. Then she said, *However, I happen to think yours is an excellent idea. I'm all for giving it a trial run and seeing what happens! I'm going to be your volunteer teacher!* We cheered like mad. ALSO, the head has agreed to us using one of the empty mobile classrooms as an office! Miss Moody's also managed to scrounge two computers and other equipment from Mr Devon in the I.T. department – and he's volunteered to help set it up! We cheered like mad again! YES! We all went round to Jay's after school and made some WHAT'S YOUR PROBLEM? posters for advertising the website around school.

Bought Cassie a de-stressing aroma pen for

her birthday. It cost loads. Good job I kept that tenner that Ian gave me for the pictures.

Friday, 24th September

19.15 Cassie was waiting for me on the front doorstep when I got home from school. I asked why she hadn't got Nolly to let her in. She said she'd tried Nolly's bell, but there was no answer. There was no sign of Nolly anywhere, though her room smelt funny — like maybe a certain person had been SMOKING and tried to cover it up with air-freshener. *P'raps she's wandered off somewhere,* said Cassie. *Sometimes old people's memories go and they start doing crazy things, like my great-granddad. He started shoplifting too — weird stuff like dog food and he didn't even have a dog.* By seven o'clock, we were getting really anxious about Nolly. Mum had phoned round all Nolly's friends but they couldn't help. Then she suddenly turned up.

Where have you been? we all yelled. *We've been worried about you!* She looked at the clock and sighed, *Och, is that the time already? I had no idea. I just went for a wee walk and sat in the park for a while.*

Mum is dead worried. She works with oldies, so knows all the signs of them going gaga. Later I asked, *Nolly, you haven't been smoking have you? 'Cos there's a strange smell in your sitting room.*

Oh, let me be, lass! she said. *All this pestering is making me ill!*

Cass liked her pen. She told me that Rachel's mum and dad got divorced a little while ago so at least she has a friend who understands how she's feeling. I said, *But I understand too.* She just shrugged.

WORRY 12 Please — don't let Nolly go gaga!

Saturday, 25th September

12.00 Cassie stayed the night. I made her a chocolate and vanilla ice cream sundae with maple syrup, smarties and chocolate flake but even that didn't cheer her up. She only had one titchy spoonful so she must be mega depressed. Went round to Jay's in the afternoon, but Cassie didn't want to come. She said it would make her feel left out and even worse than she feels now. After we'd finished making the WHAT'S YOUR PROBLEM? posters, Dan said, *We might have a problem ourselves, you know. What if no one sends any messages?* Kerry said, *We'll just have to make some up.*

Sunday, 26th September

10.20. Twinkle has just wee-weed in one of Ian's trainers. But they're so stinky he probably won't notice anyway. She looked really cute —

like she was in a bumper car!

Phoned Cass. She's staying at her friend Rachel's. Phoned Jay. No answer. Phoned Kerry, got the answerphone.

Nolly's gone round to her friend Bettie's for the day. Couldn't see any sign of ciggies in Nolly's room. I am so b-o-r-e-d.

11.05. NEWSFLASH! NEWSFLASH! NEWSFLASH! MUM IS EXPECTING A BABY!

I found her gobbling ice cubes again – so I said, *What is it with this ice cube thing?* Mum looked at Ian and said, *Are you going to tell her or shall I?* Ian grinned and said, *You tell her.* I screamed, *TELL ME WHAT!* And Mum said, *I'm going to have a baby, Finch!* Then Ian grinned, *Looks like you're gonna be a big sister, Finch.*
These are the facts:
1. Mum is eight weeks pregnant!
2. The baby's due on 4th June!
3. That's why she keeps getting cravings for ice cubes!

I hope it's a girl – and that she doesn't inherit Ian's smelly feet or swively eyes. WOW! WOW! WOW! I'm going to be a BIG SISTER! I'm gonna phone everyone and tell them.

11.35. Tried Jay, Kerry and Dan. Everyone is out! Where are they? Why haven't they invited ME?

12.40. Ian says twins run in his family! His granddad and his mum were twins. I would LOVE twin baby sisters! I'll dress them up in matching outfits and little hats with bunny ears. Molly's a good name. Molly and Polly sound nice. Or bird names – like me! Kestrel, Dove, Kite, Raven, Skylark? Or just Lark? Robin? I like Dove and Skylark. Coot? Tit? I do not think so.

17.50. Nolly just got back from the Sunday market. She's bought JEANS AND COWBOY BOOTS. She says she needs them for the line-dancing classes that she's just joined! *But what about your heart attack?* I asked. *You're supposed to be taking things gently!* She said she'd rather die dancing than in her armchair! When Mum told her about the baby she nodded and said, *Och aye, I knew that! Why did ye wait so long to tell us, lass?* She'd bought a whole load of line-dancing tapes too. Ian put them on and they all started dancing and yahooing round the kitchen. I am the only sane person in this house.

22.00. In bed. Can't stop thinking about the baby – and Mum and Ian. I think Ian really does love Mum. He'd better.

Monday, 27th September

19.00. Spent all of our breaks cleaning out the mobile classroom for the website office. Mr Devon and his crew have been brilliant setting up the WHAT'S YOUR PROBLEM? website. The main work for us will be checking the incoming mail and editing or deleting any stupid stuff and making sure that no real names go on to the screen. Miss Moody thinks that if all goes to plan it'll be ready to go on-line on Wednesday. Went round to Dan's after school and sent some test messages.

When I got home there was a strange person sitting on the doorstep. Then I realised it was Cass. She'd chopped off her hair! It's really short and spiky now. She just got fed up with her mum going on about it. She said they had a big row about it on Saturday – that's why she stayed overnight at Rachel's. While she was there she decided to cut it a bit shorter but once she'd started snipping she couldn't stop. Cassie's mum went mad bonkers when she saw it, saying, *Oh, what have you done to your lovely hair?* Honestly, you just can't please some people. Cassie's really chuffed with it though. She says it makes her feels much more interesting, like a wild child. I got used to it after a bit. It really suits her. She's quite jealous about the twins – but then she said they could turn out like her brother Leo. I hadn't thought about BOY TWINS – that wouldn't be so good.

Tuesday, 28th September

7.20. Heard Mum throwing up in the bathroom. She says she had much worse morning sickness with me though.

18.00. The test messages came through on the website OK.

All of P.S.H.E today was spent on a class discussion on the WHAT'S YOUR PROBLEM? website. Trevor asked, *What makes you lot think you're so superior and clever that you can solve everyone's problems?*

Wormbrain! So we explained very carefully that the idea is not that *we* solve problems but that other kids send in *their* suggestions. Most kids think it's a really good idea, though a few were a bit sneery. Narinder kept shooting me black looks and whispering with Mia, who spent most of the lesson doodling and twiddling her stupid hair round and round her finger. They're just jealous. Miss Moody is going to talk about it in Year Assembly tomorrow and Whole School Assembly on Friday.

Stayed behind after school and stuck up the website posters. Kerry reckons there'll be

loads of stupid messages sent in by stupid
people.

Wednesday, 29th September
Launch of the website today!
18.40 Kerry was right. Here are some of the
stupid messages sent in by stupid people.

• **My problem is that Lee Ricketts keeps picking
his nose. Get him to stop. He makes me want to
throw up. Disgusted.**
• **Who do you think you are you idoits? (someone
who can't even spell).**
• **Why don't you get a life?**
• **My problem is my maths homework (attached).
Please complete and return. Thanks, a grateful
Year Nine.**
• **My owner beats me up and and throws me round
the room. Help me! A battered teddy.**

Miss Moody told us to delete the stupid ones,
but we decided to keep the first one and
hope that Lee Ricketts sees the message and
gets the hint and stops his disgusting habit,
though we had to take out his name. Loads
more came in during lunchtime — not just
problems but answers too. Mrs Biggins in the
library complained 'cos it caused lots of

hassle with kids scrambling for computers. But Mr Devon thinks that the website is such a good idea he's volunteered to let kids use the computers in the I.T. department during the lunch hour. This is a printout of a few of the problems and answers sent in.

What?

A boy in my class picks his nose. He makes me want to throw up. What can I do? Year Nine girl.

• Throw up over him. That will teach him a lesson. D and H, Year Eight.

• I know who you mean. His finger is always excavating his nostrils. Please, please make him STOP! Year Nine girl. (We had to change this one too. It started, Do you mean Lee Ricketts?)

I pick my nose too. It's not funny – I can't stop. I think I'm addicted, though I only do it in secret. Please help me. Nose-picking addict.

• DO NOT PICK YOUR NOSE, you revolting person! Don't you know that your nose is full of germs! Do you wash your hands after? We bet not! Don't you know that every time you touch things like books and desks and paintbrushes with bogey fingers, you leave bogey germs behind? And innocent clean people like us could pick up those disgusting germs? It makes us

71

feel ill!

P.S. Your nostrils will get huge if you carry on with your horrible habit. Stop now! We will be on the lookout for someone with huge nostrils. S, D, G and M, Year Nine.

What bugs me is that some teachers are so unfair. Just because a few kids are troublemakers in lessons, we all get punished. For example, *If I hear one more groan you will all stay in.* Why? It's not fair! We didn't groan and had to stay in too!

• We agree! Goodies unite! Let's walk out next time it happens. Three fed-up girls.

I've just discovered my best friend went out with my boyfriend! What shall I do? Girl, Year Eight

• They're both creeps. You're better off without them. I'm looking for a girlfriend! What's your name? Cool Year Eight boy.

• Remember, this helpline is strictly confidential. No names please – the W.Y.P team.

My friend has cancer. She's started treatment but her hair has begun to fall out. Kids have started to make fun of her. How can people be so nasty and cruel? I think they must be sick.

• That happened to me too. But my real friends

stood by me. I've been clear for two years now.

• People who make fun like that need treatment themselves! You are a good friend. LH

By the end of our first day we'd received twenty-nine messages and loads of answers. Some were jokey, some serious and some that made you sad or angry, like the one about cancer. We all think this website is going to be really useful. EVERYONE was nattering about it.

Thursday, 30th September

7.35. There are no two socks that match in my drawer! How does Mum manage to do this? I'm going to have to wear one white sock and one black! Phoned Kerry. We've decided to set a new trend by wearing one black and one white sock each.

19.15. The website was going crazy today. There were seventy-three messages and answers! We spent all our free time in the WHAT'S YOUR PROBLEM office. It's so exciting seeing the messages coming in. Lots of teachers dropped in to see how it was getting on. Here's some of today's stuff.

Why is this website for Year Eights only? What about the rest of us? Don't we have problems? Two Year Tens.

• Yeah, we agree! Po, Laa Laa and Dipsy, Year Nine.

• As you know, the idea for this website came from Year Eight. It is in its experimental stage at present. We are not excluding any year groups. Please send in your ideas for improving the site – Miss Moody and the team.

What bugs us about teachers is the clothes they wear. One teacher has worn the same smelly old jacket every day for years – it stinks of cigarettes. Is that setting a good example? Year Ten fashion freak.

• I think teachers should have to wear uniforms like us.

• Hey, what's all this about us teachers? How about what drives teachers mad about kids? Like kids who always turn up late? Who never have a pen? Who never hand their homework in on time? Who wear their coats to lessons, and moan when you tell them to take them off – every lesson?

I'm too scared to get A's. My mates aren't bothered about school or homework and play around a lot, so I do too. My parents keep nagging me to do better. I know I could get A's but I'd lose my mates. Help.

• Lose your mates – be brave. PJ

• No one likes swots – they are sad. Your mates are

more important.

• I wish to complain. This is discrimination against us swots. We must stick together. Let's form a Society for the Protection of Swots. (S.P.S) Year Nine – founder member S.P.S.

• We would like to join S.P.S. We don't get why it's supposed to be cool to disrupt lessons. They are sad, not cool. Libra and Aquarius, Year Nine.

I have eczema – does anyone else? Fed up Year Nine.

• Yeah, me too. Do you have other allergies? I've got asthma too. Manchester City fan.

• I discovered that I'm allergic to cats. I used to get a runny nose and watery eyes. But I'm much better since Mum got rid of the cat and all our carpets. I really miss our cat, though. Cat lover.

At breaktime, me and Kerry were dashing to the loos when we got stopped by Mrs Enderby, Head of Year. She wears these suits like you see on prison warders on telly and big black lace-up prison-warder shoes. She said, *What's the meaning of this black and white sock silliness? We take pride in proper uniforms in this school. Now, please go to the cloakroom and swap*

back. *Black or white, but not one of each,
thank you very much.*

Kerry's eyes swivelled at me, like, *Who is
this mad woman?* I had to bite my tongue
and stare down at my socks. I was laughing so
much inside that I was vibrating.

Well, off you go! Quick sharp! Mrs Enderby
snapped. So off we went in this very fast mad
kind of walk – I thought I was going to
EXPLODE! The second we got to the
cloakrooms we collapsed in heaps. Only, guess
who was there? The big baby Rapunzel and
her bodyguard Narinder, playing at
hairdressers again. Narinder glared at us and
said, *Oh no – look who's arrived! I knew it
was too good to last!*

Oh, sorry, said Kerry. *We didn't realise
that this was your private cloakroom! Do we
have to get permission to use it, Your
Highnesses?*

Narinder barked, *You two have got a ruddy
cheek! Spouting on all the time about your
stupid website! It's you two who are the
problem! You think you're so clever and
important! But you haven't got a clue!*

I said, *What have we done?*

Just ignore them, said Kerry. *Or they'll go
creeping off to Miss Moody again and
whingeing that we've been bullying them.*

Rapunzel snorted, *You really think you're
IT, don't you! Well, put an S and an H in*

front of that! That's you! Kerry and me just blinked at each other as they slammed out.

Blimey, said Kerry. *Well, if they go griping to Miss Moody again, we'll tell her that they swore at us!*

I said, *I bet they still blame us though!*

We didn't change our socks. I mean, there's nothing in the school rules about it. We looked it up in the school brochure. It says white, black, or navy socks may be worn, or black or natural coloured tights. There's nothing about matching socks.

Kerry says she's really starting to fancy Dan. She was spraying herself with scent called ALLURE this morning. In maths, Jay said, *What's that pong?* And Dan said, *Dunno, but my gran smells the same.*

21.15. Cassie didn't ring back. I phoned her when I got back from school — she was out so left her a message. Have loads to tell her.

22.05. I'm not a S-H-I-T! That's horrible! I haven't done anything! It's not fair! I'm very upset about it.

Friday, 1st October
16.45. It was really weird at school! Loads of girls were wearing one black and one white sock — just like us!! Kerry and me have

started the Sock Silliness Club. (S.S.C for short!) The website was just buzzing with messages today.

I have a serious problem. I am addicted to this website. Help me please! Girl fan, Year Eight.

• Me too! I missed my clarinet lesson at lunchtime and got into trouble.

How can you tell if you've got bad breath?

• People faint when you open your mouth.

My mum still chooses my clothes and kids take the mickey.

• You are sad. Stick up for yourself.

• Why don't you ask for a clothing allowance and choose your own?

Please, please help me. My best friend made friends with some other girls and won't let me join in. Lonely Year Eight.

• Why do you want to join in? They deserve each other. Make some proper friends.

• The same thing happened to me at my last school. I've moved around a lot so I know what I'm talking about. It takes time to make a true friend. Just be friendly and not too pushy – you'll soon find a best mate.

I sent a message for Cassie. By the end of the day, I had got some really helpful answers.

I'm worried about my friend whose parents are getting a divorce. They were always having rows but it's a big shock for her. Her mum keeps crying and her little brother is throwing temper tantrums. She is really down because her dad has moved out and usually she gets on much better with her dad. Any advice? Rabbit and guinea pig lover.

• Stick by your friend – she needs you. BM, Year Nino.

• My parents were like that and I was upset when they split up. But it's much better now and I go and stay with my dad most weekends and holidays. Boy, Year Eight.

• I know just what your friend is going though. I get really depressed sometimes.

• Tell her to ring *Childline* if she can't cope. They helped me loads.

• Can you give me the number for *Childline* please? Worried Year Eight.

I've printed them out to give to Cass. The last one gave us an idea – to have a website page of helplines for different problems – like eating disorders, bullying and stuff.

Dan says Pepsi and Graeme's babies are running about now! I'm going round tomorrow morning to see them!

Half-term next week!

Saturday, 2nd October
11.45. Vacuum-cleaned Nolly's flat for

her and hung her washing out. I WILL NEVER NEVER NEVER WEAR BIG BAGGY PINK KNICKERS! She gave me £5! No sign of ciggies anywhere.

12.40. Just got back from Dan's. Thought that Jay would be there but he wasn't. BIG SIGH. The baby rabbits are SOOOOOO ADORABLE! Like dinky little toy rabbits. They kept scooting about, then dashing back to their mummy and huddling in a big furry heap next to her. Three of them are white with black blotches and ears, but the one I want looks the most like Graeme. It's white like he was, except it's got black ears and black rings round its eyes like it's wearing eye liner. It kept pushing the others out of the way so that it could get nearest to its mummy. Dan reckons it's a bossy girl rabbit. If it is, I'm going to call her Graemella. I just wanted to kidnap her and bring her home with me! But I can't have her till she's nine weeks old! Sob, sob! That's seven whole weeks!

13.10. Phoned Cass.
ME: *Hi Cass! It's me – wanna come round?*
CASS: *Oh, hiya! I was just gonna call you. Look – sorry, I can't. I'm off to Rachel's*

*— her mum's got a caravan somewhere —
near a beach anyway — and I've been
invited along too. Give you a buzz when I
get back — won't be back till next weekend,
OK? Gotta go — Mum's gonna drop me off.
See ya.*

Oh thanks, Cass!

13.20. Phoned Jay. His dad says he's gone
skateboarding.

13.25. Phoned Kerry. No answer.

14.00. In bed with Twinkle.

WORRY 13 How could Cassie agree to go off
with the boring Rachel for the whole half-
term week? We're supposed to be best
friends!

WORRY 14 Is Jay my boyfriend or not?
YES! Because:
1. He asked me out to the pictures.
2. He paid for everything and spent loads.
3. He held my hand.
4. We've been going round together for five
weeks, six days and, hold on...ten hours and
thirty minutes.
5. I caught him looking at me the other day
and I went all gooey — and he winked!
6. I can't stop secretly doodling his name,

like this:

I ♡ JAY Carter   Finch loves Jay!

I ♡ Jay

I ♡ Jay Carter

Or NO? Because:
1. He hasn't kissed me!
2. He spends every morning-break playing football.
3. He's too busy to phone and I have to call him.
4. He liked Rapunzel's drawing better than mine.
5. Maybe he likes Rapunzel more than me!
This is STUPID! I'M REALLY DEPRESSED NOW. I HATE RAPUNZEL! She is such a wimp! AND CASS HAS GONE OFF WITH RACHEL! IT'S NOT FAIR!

   Twinkle has just poohed and wee-weed over my duvet.

14.55. Ate two packets of crisps, a Wagon Wheel, a bowl of cereal and a Pot Noodle. Feel sick.

15.45. I am being driven mad by Nolly's line-dancing music blaring through my wall.

17.15. Everyone's out. Borrowed Mum's curling tongs and tried curling my hair. Tried on all my clothes to see what they would look like with curly hair.

17.40. Pinched Mum's make-up too and high heels to see what I would look like with curly hair, heels and make-up.

18.00. I look about sixteen! Wow!

18.10. Mum comes home and goes mad and says no way am I going out looking like this. Brilliant. I must look good then. Except I HAVE NOWHERE TO GO OUT TO! ALSO NO ONE TO GO WITH!

22.15. In bed. What was the point of even getting up?

23.50. Got woken up by a motorbike outside. Keep thinking about Cassie going off with Rachel for a whole week. Feel like crying. I'm not going to think about it. I'll think about Jay instead. He's wearing that green shirt I like – and jeans – he's smiling at me. I'll walk over to him – I'm wearing my black bootlegs and sparkly lilac top – he's dying to kiss me... Oh – he's vanished!

Sunday, 3rd October

11.10. Mum has just had a go at me about my room. *This isn't like you, Finch. What happened to my little alien from the planet Neat?* I told her, *Mum! That was when I was a little kid! I'm not a little girl any more. I have more important things to do than keep my room tidy! It's my room! No one should come in unless invited!* Anyway, she's the last person to talk! Her room used to be a tip – and it was me who tidied up. It's Ian who's the tidy one.

11.45. Stuck a **PRIVATE – KEEP OUT** notice on my door, with a drawing of Twinkle holding a machine gun.

12.10. I have lost Twinkle. She's in here somewhere.

12. 50. Found her in my school-bag. She has eaten half my maths book and poo-ed all over my art folder. I never had this problem with Graeme. I miss you, Graeme!

14.50. Nolly cooked dinner today – Yorkshire pudding, roast potatoes, gravy and apple crumble with custard. Yum. (Not all together.)

19.50. Things I have done since dinner:
1. Cleaned out Twinkle's hutch.
2. Experimented with three new hairstyles.

Should I chop it off like Cassie's?

3. Made up my eyes Graemella style. Ian said I looked like a panda!

4. Eaten: two peanut butter and jam sandwiches, a Mars bar, three slices of toast and marmalade.

Watched: *The Antiques Road Show.*

Is this my life? Why hasn't anyone called me?

21.50. In bed. Will Jay call me tomorrow? I'll send him a telepathic message.

Jay, Jay! Can you hear me? I'm calling you, Jay! It's me, Finch. Call me Jay! Call me tomorrow! Call me at ten, d'you hear? Call me at ten, Jay! Call me, please! I'll be waiting!

Monday, 4th October – Half-term hols!

10.10. Kerry phoned. I was a bit disappointed – I thought it was Jay. Going to meet her at the mall at one-thirty.

Right. I'm going to phone Jay NOW!

10.40. His mum answered and I heard her calling, *Jay! It's Finch, for you!* But he took ages coming to the phone, then said, *You've*

just ruined my game! I've had my soul stolen
now and I'm trapped in the Swamp of Doom.

I asked, *Are you still going out with me?*

He said, *What?* So I had to say it again.

He said, *Yeah.* But like he was desperate to
get back to his game.

I said, *So sorry to interrupt your game*
(NOT), *but I'm feeling a bit fed up, that's all.*
He said, *Right,* but like he wasn't really
listening. I could hear computer pings and
explosions in the background.

I told him, *Certain people have
been having at go at me.*

Yeah?

I told him about the trouble
with Mia and Narinder.

Oh, right.

*Well, whose side are
you on, then?* I asked.

*What? I'm not on
anyone's side.*

Well, maybe you should be on my side! I
told him. *But it sounds like you're secretly on
Mia's side!*

He said, *Why do girls always go on about
other girls? I don't get it.*

Oh, thanks a lot! I said and put the phone
down.

I knew it! I knew he liked Rapaunzel better
than me! I HATE HER! She really really bugs
me! Jay, Jay! How could you do this to me!

17.50. Kerry and me went to this new shop called LULU'S. It's got the most fantastic jewellery, hair-clips and stuff. Sabine and Sara from school were there too. I spent all my money. I bought a sparkly hairband with turquoise feathers, a sparkly purple wrist-band, some ruby hair-slides and some gold face glitter. Kerry and me tried on some tops. She fell in love with a purple glittery top but it cost £20. I had to drag her away. She was sobbing, *But this top could change my life!* We all went to THE ICE CREAM-DREAM MACHINE and had milkshakes.

20.35. Jay hasn't called! I'm not even going to think about him. I'm not going to phone him. He has to phone me and apologise.

21.45. Jay! Oh Jay! Call me! Why haven't you called me? I hate you!

22.00. I don't hate you, Jay. If I did, I wouldn't be so miz. I hate Rapunzel though.

Tuesday, 5th October

17.40. I had a big shock when I went round to Kerry's today. Mr Jones our maths teacher answered the door. I thought I'd got the wrong house. Then Kerry appeared and said,

Oh, don't mind my dad, he lives here. I said, *You never told me he was your dad.* She said, *It's not exactly the sort of thing I want people to know.*

She reckons he's the teacher with the smelly old jacket that someone moaned about on the website. It's so weird. She even calls him Mr Jones in lessons. She says all the hassle that we've had from Donna, Rapunzel and Narinder must be showing because her mum keeps asking if school is going OK. I said, *What if Miss Moody told your dad about all that trouble we got in? He'll have told your mum — and she's waiting for you to confess.* She shrugged. *Nah. My mum would just come straight out with it.* Then she told me she can't stop thinking about Dan! But the problem is he treats her like a mate and doesn't show any sign of fancying her.

We put on our new accessories, sneaked into her big sister's room, tried on her shoes, then put on some music. We pranced about till we were exhausted. Then Kerry said, *I know! Let's have a sleepover! A SPARKLE PARTY SLEEPOVER!* She's going to ask her mum about it.

19.05. Kerry phoned. The sleepover is on Saturday. She's inviting Sabine and Sara too.

Why hasn't Jay phoned me? He knows I'm upset about Narinder and Rapunzel.

20.10. Phoned Jay. His mum said that he's staying over at his cousin's.

Wednesday, 6th October

17.40. Just got back from Kerry's — and I feel TERRIBLE! Sabine and Sara were there too. We started telling them about all the grief we've had from Rapunzel and Narinder. Sara said, *Who's Rapunzel?* We explained that it's the nickname we gave Mia because of the way she fusses over her hair. They looked at one another like they were really shocked, and Sabine blurted out, *Oh no! You didn't have a go at her about her hair, did you? You shouldn't have done that because...* Then Sara screamed at her, *Shut up, Sabine! You said you wouldn't tell!*

We said, *Tell what? What's the big secret?*

Sara said, *I don't know that it's a secret exactly. It's just that my mum is friends with Mia's mum, and she told me something — but said I wasn't to spread it around, that's all.*

What's she done? asked Kerry

She hasn't done anything, Sara sighed.

You've got to tell them, said Sabine.

But I promised that I wouldn't! Sara burst out.

Right, I'll tell them, then, said Sabine. *I*

*didn't promise. I think they ought to know —
for Mia's sake.*

KNOW WHAT? TELL US! We were practically
screaming by that time.

OK — I'll tell you, said Sabine. *But I have
to warn you that it's going to make you feel
really terrible.* She took a deep breath and
said, *Mia has cancer.*

Kerry choked on the crisp she was eating. I
spluttered my cola all over the carpet.

She's having this treatment, Sabine carried
on. *But it means that she'll lose all her hair.*

Then Sara said, *Actually it started coming
out a while ago. She's really upset about it. I
can't think of anything worse, can you?
Imagine going bald.*

*Also, the treatment makes her feel really
yucky,* said Sabine. *Which is why she's off
school so much. But the doctor has told her
that it's best if she tries to carry on as
normal as possible.*

Then Sara let out this big sigh. *The
cancer's in her uterus. You know — the womb
— where babies grow?* she said. *Isn't that
awful? Her mum said it's very unusual in
young girls. But the doctor's told them that
the treatment has been very successful in lots
of cases. I don't know how Mia's carried on
like normal — I'd be going* BANANAS.

Kerry and I just blinked at each other with
our jaws dropping down to our knees almost.

I was going, *Oh! Oh, no! We didn't know! It's cringe-making! I feel like the most terrible person in the world!*

Kerry was groaning, *No you're not. I'm the most terrible person in the world! I've just remembered what I shouted at her.* Keep your hair on! Kerry let out this long howl and pulled her duvet over her head. *I'm not coming out ever! It's more than cringe-making! It's TOTAL CRINGEWORLD!*

I was remembering other things. Like me calling her hairhead — and the message on the website from someone whose friend had cancer. Was that Narinder writing about Mia? I'm one of those nasty people she wrote about! *Why didn't anyone tell us?* I howled. *Miss Moody must have known! All that stuff about Mia going through a difficult time! It's stupid keeping stuff like that secret! It's not fair!*

WORRY 15 I've got this video in my head that keeps playing and rewinding over and over. It keeps playing all the squirm-making clips of me and Kerry with Mia and Narinder. I try to switch it off, but it still keeps playing.

Thursday, 7th October
10.20. In bed. I ache from squirming. And Jay still hasn't called me either.

10.45. Kerry phoned. She says that she doesn't feel like a sparkle party sleepover right now.

11.15. Kerry phoned again. She's fed up with being miz on her own. I'm going over so we can be miz together.

11.21. Kerry phoned again. She said, *I just called Sara and found out where Mia lives. We could go round and try to explain. What d'you think?* I said, *It would be totally cringe-makingly embarrassing. Anyway, they'd probably just tell us to get lost.* She said, *Yeah, that's what I thought too.*

18.00. Spent the whole afternoon under Kerry's duvet cringeing about it. Kerry sighed, *Well, she's not Rapunzel any more, that's for sure.* I cringed *Don't! You're making it cringe-makingly worse! Cringe! Cringe!* She said, *We have to do this — it's our punishment — we have to cringe to death in Cringeworld.*

Friday, 8th October
13.00. Kerry came round this morning. We got under my duvet and did Cringeworld again. I said, *I don't think I can face Mia ever again. It's going to be terrible going back to school.* Kerry said *I know. I might*

have to run away and become a hermit.
I told her they don't have hermits any
more. She said, *I'll be a nun then.* I said, *I
thought you fancied Dan – nuns aren't
allowed boyfriends.* She howled, *Oh, why
is life so cruel!* Then she sat up and
said, *It's no good! We can't go on like
this! We've got to pull ourselves together! We
need help!* She grabbed her bag and took out
a monster packet of mini Mars Bars
and said, *We are going to have to
eat all of these.* I told her, *I can't –
it'll make me sick!* Kerry said, *I know.
And that will be our punishment for being so
evil. It's important that we suffer.*

I feel sick.

15.50. I still feel sick. And I've got a sore
throat.

19.45. I think I've got a cold coming. SHUT
UP! SHUT UP! It's only a cold! Think what
Mia is going through!

Saturday, 9th October
9.50. I'm too ill to write. My head aches. I
think it must be flu. Also it would help if Ian
stopped all that drilling and sawing and
banging outside my window. Mum says he's
making a playhouse for the baby. I'd have
loved a playhouse.

12.30. Kerry phoned. She's ill, the same as me. The sparkle party is definitely cancelled.

13.10. Nolly brought some ice cream for my throat. Nice, nice Nolly.

16.45. Mum's just come in and complained about all the tissues on the floor. Can't she see that I'm too ILL AND DEPRESSED to reach the bin?

Sunday, 10th October
10.50. I'm all stuffed up, my throat aches and I have flaking red nostrils. My hair is all greasy. I have spilt cough mixture down my pyjamas. I'm under my duvet on the settee watching my old *Chitty Chitty Bang Bang* video with Twinkle and my old teddy, Eddy. I am the nastiest sad person in the world.

11.15. Jay called round! I tried to hide under my duvet. He said, *Hey, you look terrible!* Which really cheered me up. Not. He wanted to know if I'd like to go swimming with him this afternoon! Why couldn't he have asked me yesterday! I said, *Sorry that I slammed the phone down on you.* He said, *Did you?* Then he started looking at me very strangely

– and bent over me – and I was thinking, *He's going to kiss me! He's going to kiss me!* But he just grinned and said, *Hey – did you know that you've got guinea-pig droppings in your hair?* He laughed and picked them out for me. He smelt really nice. Sort of bike oil and fresh air. I felt all gooey again. Then I told him about Mia. He said, *Wow, poor Mia. That's tough. I bet you feel bad now. So why don't you just make it up with her, then?* Which made me feel even worse. Then he held my hand – and started to lean forward with kissy lips! And I was going totally melty-floaty – when in marched Mum saying, *How about some ice cream for your sore throat, Finch? Would you like some too Jay?* AGH! So we had some ice cream, then Jay said, *Well, gotta go, s'posed to be meeting up with Dan – see you at school, then.* Jay was DEFINITELY going to kiss me! I'm just going to just lie here imagining Jay kissing me.

11.25. Mum wants to know why there's a neat little pile of Twinkle poos on the coffee table.

11.45. Mum wants to know why I need kitchen roll, scissors and sticky tape. Explain that I need to make guinea-pig nappies. Do not think guinea-pig poo in hair is very attractive.

12.30. I am SWOONING from imaginary snogging.

12.45. Yummy smells wafting from Nolly's kitchen.

13.00. Nolly asks, *Can ye manage a wee bitta dinner, lass? Roast chicken and tatties! I've made some of your favourite stuffing specially – and choccy pud too.* Nod weakly.

14.15. Phoned Kerry and told her about Jay.

15.35. Helped Nolly finish off choccy pud.

16.30. Mum says I'm well enough to go to school tomorrow. I'm not going on my own! Not without Kerry!

16.35. Phone Kerry. She has promised to drag herself to school even if she is dying. That's what mates are for.

20.20. Kerry phoned and asked if I thought if anyone would notice if we wore our duvets to school. Cass hasn't phoned like she promised.

Monday, 11th October
19.45. A REALLY ANNOYING AND HORRIBLE DAY.
1. THE ANNOYING BIT
No Mia at school today. Narinder was going

round with Donna Siddley. And they were both wearing one black sock and white sock each! They were copying us! We could not believe it! Then later, as we were queuing up outside the geography room, Donna hissed from behind, *Copy-cats! Can't you think for yourselves?* I turned round and said, *Uh? What?* She said, *It was me who started this black and white sock fashion! So just try thinking for yourself, why don't you?*

Kerry, said, *No, you didn't! It was us! It's our Sock Silliness Club! And no way do we want you as a member!*

Donna snorted, *You are so completely sad! You're sick too! I know what you've been saying to poor Mia!* She shoved her face up to me and sneered, *Anyway, people with legs like your's oughtn't to draw attention to them. They look like bits of white string dangling down!*

I was so mad! *Better than having great fat elephant legs, Jumbo!* I yelled. Then, Mr Sowerbutts – who had sneaked up behind me – roared, *That's quite enough of that, Finch Penny!* And made me wait for all the others to lead in first! And he gave me an ear-bashing after. I tried to explain about the black and white sock thing. He sighed, *Really, isn't this all a bit childish? Arguing about socks!* He didn't understand at all. It was so unfair! Donna and Narinder kept looking at us and whispering all day. At least we could escape from them at lunchtime to the W.Y.P office. The website was flooded with messages. Kids had been sending mail over half-term. There were loads of **What drives us mad about teachers,** and quite a lot of **What drives us mad about kids,** from teachers. Cheek! We're wondering if we should allow those. Why don't teachers organise their own website? There were so many emails that Miss Moody brought in two Year Nines to help out. They were really pushy, though.

Kerry and me wanted to email our problem about the sock thing and people who copy other people's ideas. But everyone would know it was us. Anyway, it's too feeble compared to other kids' problems. Some of the problems start getting to you, like the one from a boy in Year Eight who has terrifying nightmares about vampires and is too scared to go to sleep.

WISH 13 I wish that Donna Siddley gets sock-poisoning and her feet drop off and her bushy eyebrows grow longer and longer so I don't have to see her sneery face or her ugly fat legs.

2. THE HORRIBLE BIT

Just as I got home, Cass phoned. She said, *Hi! Just testing from my new mobile. Can you meet me in Cosmo's in about fifteen minutes? Got heaps of news.* (Cosmo's is a really trendy coffee bar!) I told her that I hadn't got any money. She said, *Don't worry about it.*

When I got there, I couldn't see her. Then I spotted someone waving. Someone with spiky hair, a pale white face and black eyeliner. She was dressed all in black with black lace-up boots. When I got closer, I could see she'd had her ears pierced too – three studs in each ear. I couldn't believe it! How could Cass have changed so much in two weeks? Cass says it's the Gothic look – and she's one of the four Gothic Girls – her, Rachel and two others called Vix and Pip. They all started together as new girls in the same class. It was Vix's idea. They change into it after school. I could see Cass's uniform sticking out from her rucksack. She kept saying, *What d'you think? It's cool, isn't it?* I couldn't stop staring. She'd pass for sixteen easily.

I said, *Did your mum let you pierce your ears, then?* She said, *No way! The four of us had them done together. Anyway, it's no big deal. Loads of girls at school have them –*

though we're not allowed to wear them in school. She shoved a menu at me and said, *Choose anything you like – I've got enough money*. I had a double almond latte and cherry and chocolate mousse cheesecake. It cost £6.20! I gave her the printout of the school website question that I sent in on parents and divorce, and the answers. She said, *Oh, cool,* and shoved them in her bag – without even looking at them. Then she grinned, *Hey – guess what? I've got a boyfriend!* This is what else she told me:

1. Her boyfriend is Rachel's brother. His name's Oliver but everyone calls him Olly.
2. He is fifteen!
3. They snogged loads when they were staying at the caravan.
4. Her dad gave Cassie the mobile so they can keep in touch.
5. Every time she visits her dad he gives her money.

Cass said the Gothic Girls go round together all the time. There are different groups in school – like The Swots, The Sporties, The Posers and The Horsey Girls. She went on and on about St Monica's and Rachel and the caravan and how hilarious it had been. So I told her all about school too, about the website and Kerry and Mia and Cringeworld but she wasn't really listening. Her mobile rang about a million times –

which she kept answering and nattering away while I just sat waiting. It was S☺ annoying. Then she kept peering through the window, saying, *Olly should be here by now.*

I was feeling really fed up so I said that I thought Rachel was a bit boring. And Cass said, *No – she's really funny.* So I said, *Don't you miss me then? We are still best friends, aren't we?* And she said, *Yeah. But I can't not make new friends, can I? I can't just go round on my own?*

Then Olly the boyfriend turned up. He's tall, skinny and spotty and has earrings all round his ears and spiked hair too. I said, *Hi, I'm Finch.* He mumbled, *Yeah, cool,* and sat slouched in his chair looking totally bored – like he was waiting for me to go. So I went. I'm feeling all miz now. I wanted Cass to be miz about missing me – but she wasn't. Seeing her like that made me feel like a little kid. It's like Cass isn't Cass any more. All that wailing about how she was going to miss me and never make new friends! She has LOADS!

WORRY 16 Is Cass still my best friend? Me and Kerry have decided to stop wearing odd socks now that everyone is copying us. We are going to wear navy blue knee-socks instead. Kerry says they are tres French. Oui! Ooh-la-la! So there, Fat Legs and Narinder!

Tuesday, 12th October

16.45. In P.S.H.E today, Miss Moody got the class talking about the website and asked for suggestions for improving it. Trevor said it's disorganised and needs a system to sort out the problems into subjects, like **Parents, Health, School** and so on. This is the same Trevor who was rubbishing it when we started! Now he thinks he's an expert!

Anyhow, we had already thought about that. We're planning an index page with lots of subjects, like FRIENDS, HEALTH, SCHOOL, BULLYING and so on, that kids can just click on to and get advice. There wasn't a single person who hadn't logged on to the website, though. Most kids think it's brilliant. Narinder was sending death-ray looks at me and Kerry all the time, and Donna was looking smug. But not for long, HA! HA! Because Mrs Enderby came in and said, *Excuse me for interrupting Miss Moody, but could I just ask everyone who is wearing odd black and white socks to stand up, please?* Well, that was nearly half the class — including Donna Fat Legs, but not me, Kerry, Jay or Dan. Then she announced, *Let me make it absolutely clear to one and all that the wearing of odd socks is definitely not in accordance with school uniform. Those who continue with this sock silliness will lose two house points for each occasion they come to school wearing them. I'm pleased to see* that we have some students who have more sense than to follow the common herd. Let that be an end to it. We turned round and smiled at Donna. The look on her face! It was so funny!

After she'd left, Miss Moody said, There is something else I want to tell you today. As you will have noticed, Mia Russell has been away from school. The reason is that she has been having treatment for cancer. Lots of people gasped and started whispering. Miss Moody carried on, However, the good news is that her mother tells me the treatment has a very good rate of success and Mia is responding well. However it does have side effects, like making her feel rather poorly and sick. Also, she has now lost her hair. It will grow back, but meanwhile I'm sure you will all be understanding and supportive when she returns to school next week.

Miss Moody had brought a get-well card and passed it round the class for everyone to sign. All the time, Narinder was giving us the evil eye. I was desperately trying to think what to write, like, It's all been a big mistake! Let's make up! Me and Kerry aren't the horrible nasty people you think we are! We had no idea that you were ill. We thought that

103

you were just having a go at us — and we were only trying to stick up for ourselves. Now we feel TERRIBLE! We are TRULY TRULY SORRY about everything. So — what d'you think? But that would have taken up most of the card. And I wasn't going to give Fat Legs the satisfaction of seeing me squirming. Other kids had written, BE BRAVE! and GOOD LUCK, HOPE YOU'LL SOON BE BACK. In the end Kerry wrote, *We didn't know and we are* **TRULY SORRY**, and we both signed our names under it. We were feeling total creeps by then. As we filed out, Narinder glared, *You've got a ruddy nerve signing the card. You couldn't care less!* I said, *Look wait...* She hissed, *Get lost Bird-brain!*

We spent all our breaks and an hour after school sorting the WHAT'S YOUR PROBLEM? email, but still haven't caught up. Miss Moody says she's thinking about involving kids from other years! We said, *But it's OURS! We don't want anyone else barging in!* At least the website takes my mind off Mia for a bit.

Wednesday, 13th October

17.00. Jay sent me a note in music. It said: Like the socks — very sexy! XX. I nearly fainted. When I turned to look at him, he winked. I'm keeping the note in my bra. Every time I think about him, I go all wobbly. Kerry keeps sighing over Dan and tossing her hair and laughing hysterically at all his jokes — a bit too much actually. Maybe that's what's putting him off.

18.45. Mum wants to know if I've seen Nolly because she's not in her flat — and she's left her alarm button behind. I said I hadn't seen her since last night. She asked, *Didn't you see her when you got home from school?* I told her that I didn't look. She said, *Why not? You always pop in to to see her after school?* Like it's all MY fault.

19.20. We can't find Nolly! It's all my fault!
20.00. Panic over. Ian found her in the pub on the corner playing darts with a man with a bushy white beard. Mum is really cross with her and went on about the alarm button and how she's supposed to be taking things slowly. Nolly didn't understand what the fuss was all about and sighed, *I'm seventy-three, Debbie! Not three, lass!! I haven't lost my marbles yet!*

Thursday, 14th October
7.25. Kerry phoned to say she's going to wear

mascara today to make herself more alluring to Dan. I've got to tell her if it's too obvious because we're not allowed to wear make-up at school.

17.15. Kerry was fluttering her eyelashes like mad today. Dan said, *Have you got something in your eye or what?*

We have two more computers in the W.Y.P office – not new ones, but they're OK.

There were some really tragic messages on the website today from a Year-Nine girl whose baby brother was rushed into hospital and is in intensive care and a Year-Eight boy whose mum is in a wheelchair – he has to do everything for her. Even take her to the toilet! I'M NEVER GOING TO COMPLAIN ABOUT ANYTHING AGAIN.

Friday, 15th October

7.20. Why does Ian have to sing along with the radio every morning? And if he jumps on to the chair strumming the frying pan like a guitar again I shall scream. AAAAAAH!

18.00. At lunchtime, Jay stood behind me when I was sitting at the computer and put his hands on my

shoulders! I nearly tingled to death. I went to
Kerry's after school. We've invented a new
game called Slagging-off World. It's a bit like
Cringeworld, when we lay under the duvet, but
instead of cringeing, we slag people off.
People like Donna Siddley mainly. Like she
could have her own fashion catalogue, selling
stuff for bushy eyebrows, like care-kits with
mini lawn mowers for trimming them, shampoo
for eyebrow dandruff, eyebrow clips, or beads
for plaiting into her eyebrows. Also special
corsets for fat legs to squeeze them to normal
size. Then we slagged off ourselves a bit over
Mia. Kerry says the strain of it all must be
really showing because even her mum noticed
she hasn't been her usual self. She still keeps
saying stuff like, *How's school going? Are you
getting on OK? You would let me know if you
had any problems, wouldn't you?*

We phoned Jay up and asked if him and
Dan would like to come skating with us at the
Rollerdrome tomorrow. They said *YES!* Why do
girls have to do all the work? Kerry says she's
going for the full works to make
herself alluring for Dan tomorrow.
I'm going round to help.

Saturday, 16th October
9.15. Woken up by Ian
singing at the top of his
voice in the shower, *Baby*

love, oh baby love. Then just as I'm pouring milk on my cornflakes, he comes in and asks Mum, *What d'you think about breastfeeding, love? I've been reading up on it — breast milk's definitely best for babies.* Pl-eee-se! Not when I'm eating! He's obsessed with babies! They've got a list of baby names on the kitchen pinboard, but Ian's are really boring, like Michael and William, Anna and Clare. I like some of Mum's, like Lily and Luke.

What am I going to wear for the Rollerdrome, then?

9.45. Not going! Jay just phoned. Both him and Dan have got colds now, the same as us. He sounded really bad. Phoned Kerry. We're going to meet up at the mall.

10.10. Kerry phoned. She's in big trouble and has been grounded because she's been using her dad's computer to browse the kids' chatlines. Now her dad's had this scary phone bill. From now on, she's not allowed to use it without permission.

Tried phoning Cassie, but couldn't get a peep from her mobile. She's probably worn it out. Tried her at home. Left a message on the answerphone. Bet she's out with all her mates. Unlike ME. Nolly had her line-dancing tapes belting out again. It's sort of catching — you can't stop walking round in time to it. She's started to teach me the steps. It's quite good fun ak-tchoooly! Yee-ha!

Went shopping with Mum at Sainsbury's. Cleaned out Twinkle's hutch. Tried out Mum's peach facescrub and facepack. Watched TV. Played rummy with Nolly.

Sunday, 17th October

19.45. Another boring day. Even Twinkle and Nolly have more exciting lives than me. Nolly's gone on an outing to a steam-engine museum.

Monday, 18th October

Jay and Dan were off school today, but Mia was back. She was wearing a wig. It looked quite real. Not as beautiful as her real hair, just brown and shoulder-length. We didn't know what to do – ignore her or smile, but then she might have thought we were staring. In the end, we decided to keep a low profile, but at the same time show sympathetic *How-awful-for-you. We-think-you-are-really-brave* expressions. We thought about smiling encouragingly and practised in the cloakroom mirror but Kerry reckoned it could easily be mistaken for smirking. So we didn't bother. My face aches now. Every time I glanced over, Narinder caught me and glared. Donna kept fussing over Mia, like she was incapable of even pulling out her own chair.

At lunchtime we escaped to the W.Y.P office — and got a **BIG SHOCK**. Miss Moody had brought in two Year Ten girls — Angela Harrington and Sophie Hart. *We hope you don't mind us coming along,* said Angela. *Miss Moody thought we might be useful.* Then Sophie said, *We think the website is a great idea — so much so that we'd like to be involved, and we're full of ideas for improving it.* Me and Kerry could not believe it! Miss Moody must have seen our faces because she went, *Well, you have to admit, we could certainly do with some help — there are always lots of messages on Monday. We'll see how it goes, shall we?* Except they didn't just help out. They started discussing it like we weren't there, then asking stuff like, *Wouldn't it be better if you put that here, and did it like this...*

We phoned Jay and Dan after school. They are mad about it. Jay says his temperature went up to **103** yesterday. He says he misses me!

Tuesday, 19th October
Jay and Dan still off. Really missed them in the W.Y.P office. It's never going to be the

same again! Big-head Angela and Bossy Sophie were there AGAIN saying really annoying things like, *We think you've done wonderfully well with the website but for it to be truly fair and taken seriously it ought to have input from all year groups.* Kerry was sitting behind her acting like she was about to throw up. Later, we went to tell Miss Moody about how we felt. *It's OUR website! We don't want anyone barging in and taking it away from us! And what will happen when Jay and Dan get back?* Miss Moody says she'll discuss it with us when they're back, but that we need to think about changes and involving more people, maybe having different teams from all years and a duty rota so that we have some free time. That way we'd only have to do one or two sessions a week. Kerry and me said, *But it's OUR idea!* Miss Moody just smiled, *I know – and it's a very good one. So good that all the year groups are using it. So we really have to think about letting all years help run it.*

IT'S NOT FAIR!

WORRY 17 They're trying to take over our website.
It wasn't very nice at morning break either. It was wet break so we were in the classroom. All the girls were round Mia, being extra friendly and chatty to her. Kerry said,

Shall we sort of wander over and loiter and join in with a bit of casual chat?

Like what? I asked. Kerry went, I dunno – something like, 'Your wig looks great – does it itch?'

I said, How about, 'It really suits you – you look fantastic.'

Kerry went, Okay-ish. But it sounds a bit like sucking up. I think we should put ourselves down a bit and add something like, 'Unlike me with my thin lips.' Then you could say, 'Unlike me with my sticky-out ears.'

I said, My ears don't stick out!

Kerry said, I'm not saying they do stick out. It's just something to say. Or you could say, 'Unlike me with my skinny legs.'

Then the bell went and we didn't say anything. My ears don't stick out! Do they? And why does everyone keep going on about my skinny legs?

WISH 14 I wish I knew how to make it up with Mia.

Wednesday, 20th October

18.50. I hate Donna Siddley! She is a **bully**! I was on my own in the morning because Kerry was at the dentist. When I came out of the loo at break I saw her coming in. I went to wash my hands when she suddenly grabbed me from behind and shoved me up against the wall. She hissed, *Right! You're going to say sorry!* I said *What?* She said, *You heard, Bird-brain!! No one calls me Jumbo and gets away with it! Now say SORRY.* So I just mumbled, *Sorry.* Then she sneered, *Didn't sound like you meant it! Say it again!* So I did. Then she said, *You are sick! Picking on people with cancer! I'll be watching you — so be very, very careful.* And then she let me go. I was shaking afterwards. I'm not going to the cloakrooms on my own again.

Jay and Dan were back today though, which helped. Dan says I ought to tell someone. Oh, yeah? That will make it worse! Not only will I be the person who laughed at someone with cancer, I'll be a sneak too. And Jumbo will be after me. She'd only deny it anyway. Me and Kerry are going to stick together at all times. At least I can get away at lunchtimes. It was back to normal in the W.Y.P office today, thank goodness. Went round to Kerry's after school. We did Slagging-off World about Donna again. The sparkle party sleepover is going to be this Saturday at Kerry's. Sara and Sabine are coming too.

19.20. Can't stop thinking about Donna. She really BUGS ME! Who does Jumbo Siddley think she is? I'm feeling angry now.

19.40. VERY VERY ANGRY! And a bit scared. ⊙K. Very scared.

20.05. Jay phoned! He said he just wanted to know if I was ⊙K! He said to let him know if there was any more trouble. I said, *What would you do then?* He said, *I could show you some karate moves.* He must love me then!

Thursday, 21st October

18.50. Miss Moody brought some more kids to the office today — Year Nines mainly. Kids she thinks would make useful team members! They asked questions and we had to show them what we do. Afterwards, Dan said, *Maybe it wouldn't be such a bad idea to have rotas.* Me and Kerry went, *WHAT!* And Jay said, *Well, we need to take a break sometimes — me and Dan never get time to play football these days.* We both went *WHAT!* again. Kerry rolled her eyes and snorted. *That's all you ever think about!* So Jay really does like football more than me! Went round to Kerry's after school. We were feeling so fed up we sneaked into her dad's study and wrote some fake messages to W.Y.P.

WHAT BUGS US is Donna Fat Legs Siddley! Not only does she think she's IT but she is a copy-cat and a bully. Today she was doing some serious menacing in the girls' loos. She should be punished by being made to walk round naked wearing only her smelly black and white socks.

Mia, we are feeling like TOTAL MONSTERS about everything we said and have cringed to death about it a zillion times. It was all a HUGE MISTAKE! HONESTLY! SORRY! SORRY! SORRY! Please, please get better. Finch and Kerry.

We didn't send them of course, but we felt ten times better. Then we heard Kerry's dad come home and Kerry was going. Quick! Quick! Delete them and shut down! He'll do his nut if he finds us in here!

Donna was smirking at me in a really menacing way all day at school.

Friday 22nd October

16.35. Total total squirmy-cringe-cringe embarrassment today. Eeeek! Eeeek! Eeeek! I can't even THINK about it without eeeking. In the middle of morning registration Miss Moody came to our class and asked to see Kerry and me. She was holding a piece of paper in her hand and demanded, *Right, you two! I want an explanation for this!* The piece of paper was a printout of our fake emails! Somehow they had been sent instead of deleted! Eeeek!

Miss Moody marched us to the office where we had this long lecture. We tried to explain that it was all a mistake but we felt so stupid! I had to tell her about Donna in the loos and everything. In maths Mia and Narinder were called out too – then Miss Moody sent for us again. She asked them if they had anything to say to us. And Narinder said, *Well, they keep on staring at us.* So we said, *We weren't staring! Only trying to look friendly, because we felt so bad about all that had happened.* And I told them how Donna had pounced on me in the loos and nearly strangled me. Narinder looked quite shocked and blurted out, *That was nothing to do with us! I can't stand Donna! Neither of us can – she just follows us around!* Miss Moody said, *Well, Mia, I think that both Finch and Kerry do honestly feel sorry about their behaviour. Maybe there's been a misunderstanding on both sides.* And she showed them our fake email which sort of proved that we meant it. Mia looked surprised but Narinder just glared. Miss Moody said, *Now I'm hoping that you can all make a fresh start.* And she made us do the handshaking thing again – which was so cringey. She said she'd be talking to Donna later.

Afterwards, Kerry said, *Do you think they believed us?* I said, *We'll find out soon enough. If they keep staring and being friends with Donna, we'll know.* The trouble was, we were too nervous to look to see if they were staring 'cos they would have thought we were staring at them again. It's really hard not to look at people. Your eyes keep wandering. We were waddling around like penguins and staring at our feet going eeeek! eeeek! for the rest of the day. It was worse with Miss Moody in the W.Y.P office 'cos I really like her — but I feel like I've let her down over the Mia thing and those fake emails. Even though she's been nice to me I feel totally STUPID!

Kerry came back with me after school. Nolly gave us some line-dancing lessons. It stopped us cringing for a bit. We've decided to make it a sparkly line-dancing sleepover. Phoned Sara and Sabine to tell them.

19.05. Kerry phoned. She's deleted all traces of our fake emails from her dad's computer. She thinks that in her rush to shut down her dad's computer she accidentally moved them to the outbox. Then, when her mum logged on to check for messages, it sent them. She's sure her dad hasn't noticed or he'd have said something.

Saturday, 23rd October

8.50. Had a ~~weird~~ dream that Ian was a teacher at school. I was calling him Mr Tanner. It was a science lesson and he was telling us that breast milk was best for babies. He had these diagrams on a big chart with a big arrow pointing at a sad-looking skinny baby with a label saying BOTTLE-FED BABY and next to it a giant smiling baby labelled BREASTFED BABY. Then Mum walked in with these two enormous twin babies attached to her bosoms! The twins were wearing school uniforms.

10.25. YES! No school! No Donna Siddley! Yippee! Sparkly sleepover at Kerry's! DOUBLE YIPPEE! It starts at six! Cleaned Nolly's flat for her again and did her some ironing. She gave me £7.50 this time! Gonna take my bunny jim-jams, slippers, hot-water bottle, Ian's smelly sleeping bag, and all my sparkle stuff, etc. Going to meet Kerry, Sabine and Sara at LULU'S at two o'clock.

12.10. Kerry just phoned. She was screaming, *I am going to murder my mum. I mean it! Why can't she mind her own flipping business! You are never gonna believe what she's just done!*

This is major Cringeworld stuff! She's invited
Mia and Narinder to our sleepover! I said, But
she can't! Anyway, how could she do that?

What happened was that Kerry went with
her mum to the supermarket to get the food
for the sleepover – and they bumped into Mia
and her mum! And it turns out that both
their mums know each other from their
evening classes. Kerry's mum had heard all
about Mia and her illness from
her mum, but didn't realise that
Kerry and Mia were in the same
class. Then Kerry's mum starts
nattering on about, *Oh Kerry,*
wouldn't it be nice if Mia
came to the sleepover too!
Kerry knew that no way would
Mia want to come to our
sleepover. But Mia's mum started
nodding and saying to Mia what a lovely idea
and how it would do her good as she was a
bit down at the moment. Kerry said her eyes
practically exploded from all the signals she
was trying to send to her mum. She was
hissing, *Just leave it, Mum! She doesn't want*
to come! And Mia was muttering, *Mum! I*
don't want to go! I'm going round to
Narinder's! But Kerry's mum just steam-
rollered on, saying, *Well, bring Narinder too!*
You'd like that, wouldn't you, Kerry? Mia
stomped off then.

I told Kerry, *Don't worry! They won't come. No way!* Kerry said, *Yeah, I know — but I could strangle my mum.* It was DOUBLE DOUBLE CRINGEWORLD.

Haven't heard from Cass. Over a week now since I left her a message. Well, if she's too busy to phone, then so am I.

Sunday, 24th October

THE WEIRDEST WEIRDEST THING HAS HAPPENED. Yesterday afternoon me, Kerry, Sara and Sabine met up in LULU'S looking for sparkly stuff for our sleepover. Kerry was telling them about the embarrassing supermarket thing with Mia and her mum when suddenly Sara started eyeballing me — because right behind us were Mia and Narinder! They were trying on all this sparkly stuff too! Kerry was making panic faces, like, *Oh no! Don't say they are going to come!* Next thing they spot us. And Narinder snorts, *Don't worry! We're not coming to your sleepover. We're having our own.* Then just as they start to turn away, Sabine hisses at me and Kerry, *This is so stupid!* And she grabs me and Kerry and drags us after them calling, *Mia! Wait!* As Mia and Narinder turn round Sabine announces, *I think Finch and Kerry have something to tell you.* Then she glares at us, *Go on, then! Say something!* So I mumbled, *Look, we're really, really sorry about* everything that's happened – we feel terrible about it. Maybe we can sort of start all over again? Then Kerry starts gabbling, *Yeah, and I'm really sorry about what happened this morning! It's all my mum's fault! She can be really pushy sometimes. I'm gonna throttle her later.*

Mia shrugged, *Oh that. Didn't you know? That was all set up by our mums.*

Kerry blinked, *WHAT!*

Mia said, *Look, my mum guessed something was going on at school. She kept on and on about it. So on Friday I told her about it but explained that it had been sorted. But she was really shaken up because she's friendly with your mum, so she told her about it too. Somehow they came up with this stupid idea that if they got us together we could all be friends or something. So they set up that so-called accidental meeting in the supermarket. I sussed that out after a few secs. My mum's admitted it all. And I've never been so humiliated in my life!*

Kerry was gasping. *What! What!*

We stood there, blinking like idiots. So I asked, *Who's going to your sleepover, then?*

We haven't decided yet, said Narinder.

Then I looked at Kerry and she looked at me, and I said, *Well, Sabine and Sara are*

*coming to ours. Look — you could come if you
wanted. Couldn't they, Kerry?* Kerry nodded
and said, *Yeah, but only if you wanted to.*
Narinder looked at Mia. Mia frowned.
Narinder shrugged like she couldn't care less.

I said, *At least it would please both your
mums, wouldn't it?* And Kerry said, *Yeah, and,
well — it would sort of make us feel a bit
better too.*

Mia looked at Narinder. Then Sabine cried,
*Right! That's agreed then! Sorted! They're
coming! And you can't change your minds!*

Only for a bit, said Narinder.

So they came to our sleepover. There wasn't
really room for six. Kerry's got one of those
bunk beds with a single on the top and a
double settee bed on the bottom which we'd
opened up. In the end we
tugged all the mattresses
on to the floor and
made one huge bed.
Mia's mum sent this
carrier bag bulging
with popcorn and
crisps, chocolates and
stuff. It was awful. No
one was talking — except
stupid stuff, like, *Oh, I just
love Hoola Hoops.*

Then Sabine said, *You
didn't finish telling us*

about what happened this morning in the supermarket. Kerry groaned, *Don't remind me! It was TOTAL CRINGEWORLD!* And she dived under her duvet — then did this Total Cringeworld performance on the supermarket thing, doing all the voices and the expressions of her mum and Mia's mum, and Mia and herself. It was SO FUNNY — everyone was in hysterics! Mia said, *It was Total Cringeworld for me too!*

Then we took turns doing Cringeworld. Sara did one about the time one of her big brother's mates came round. She says he's dead good-looking and she really fancied him. She was making a strawberry milkshake so she offered to make him one too. She was sucking her's, trying to look attractive, but it went down the wrong way and she was spluttering so much that all this pink stuff came snorting out of her nose — and splattered all over him and his glass! We just collapsed in a big heap going, *Oh cringe! Oh cringe!*

In the end Mia and Narinder stayed the night. Mia was wearing her wig but said she hates it because it's hot and itchy, so she's thinking about not bothering. She took it off and we all tried it on. Then we put on our sparkly gear. Sparkly nail varnish (different colour for each finger and toe), bangles, earrings, chokers, face glitter and tops. We had enough stuff to share with Mia and Narinder. Then we pigged out on the goodies in the carrier bag. At the bottom were six parcels in glittery wrapping from Mia's mum. Inside were sparkly wig hats! Sara had gold, Sabine red, Narinder blue, Mia silver, Kerry purple and I had pink. It was brilliant! We gave Mia the card we'd made for her, saying WE ARE TRULY TRULY SORRY that we were so horrible to you.

We'd done all the letters in glitter. After that we did some sparkly line-dancing. We were still nattering at midnight. I told Mia I thought she was amazingly brave 'cos I'd be dead depressed if I lost all my hair. She said she cried loads at first but her mum was even more upset and keeps all the hair in a special box. She said she got quite angry with her mum sometimes because it made her feel worse to see her crying. Anyhow, the doctor is really pleased with her test results. Sara said, *What does a uterus look like, exactly?* Kerry said, *It's like this*, and drew this great wobbly shape in the air, and we all fell about laughing. So Mia set us a competition to draw one. Then she collected them and spread them out. Kerry's looked like an alien with big pop eyes. Sara's was like a light bulb. Narinder's was like a bike saddle. Sabine's was like a giant slug, and mine was like a frog. We laughed so much it hurt. Mia said that what helped her was to pretend she was a warrior princess with the power to zap her enemies. So she imagined that the cancer cells were her enemies and she sent death-rays, killing them off one by one, and it really helped.

Then we played, *There were six in the bed and the bossy one said, Roll over! Roll over! And they all rolled over and one fell out! There were five in the bed and the bossy one said...* Except the one who rolled over had to dash round to the other side and get in again, so it went on for ever. Till Kerry's dad knocked on the wall and shouted. *Settle down! Settle down! It's one thirty a.m, you know!* So Kerry dived under the cover to do Cringeworld about her dad, but she lost her sparkly wig and started feeling around for it. That started us all off screaming again. She cried, *It's OK — I've found it!* But when she turned the light on she'd got her knickers on her head. So we all put knickers on our heads. It's the weirdest thing. On Friday we were deadly enemies. Last night we were laughing our knickers off!

125

The next sleepover is going to be at Narinder's. We are going to be WARRIOR PRINCESSES. We're going to make costumes for it.

Mum says Cass phoned yesterday. Phoned her at her mum's, but her mum said, *She's at her dad's* and gave me the number. Got the answerphone so left her a message. Have lost her mobile number.

Monday, 25th October

16.45. The look on Donna Siddley's face when she saw me and Kerry with Mia and Narinder! Like she couldn't believe her eyes. She was going round with Carmen and Kayleigh today. Mia didn't wear her wig today. She wore a pink and blue stripy beany hat. For the first time me and Kerry didn't really feel like rushing off to the W.Y.P office at lunchtime. We just wanted to hang around with Mia, Narinder, Sara and Sabine. Maybe team rotas aren't such a bad idea.

17.50. Ian's in a right old mood. He just had a go at me! *Your mum's been on her feet all day and she's not feeling too well either. The last thing she wants is to come home to a sink full of mugs to wash!* I didn't leave them for her to wash! I was going to do them before she got home! And yeah – I'd planned to clear the table too! Now he's shoved all my warrior princess drawings in the magazine rack! They are completely ruined!

WORRY 18 I forgot all about Mum! I'm going to be more helpful.

19.10. Made Mum put her feet up on the sofa and made her a cup of tea.

Tuesday, 26th October

19.00. Mia, Narinder, Sabine and Sara came back here after school and we planned out the Warrior Princess Sleepover. I'm going to be Princess Zarida. My special powers will be **invisibility** and **hypnotism**. Kerry is going to be Princess Astra with the power of **X-ray vision** and **spring-loaded boots** so she can leap hundreds of feet into the air. My costume will have a very short lacy skirt with jagged edges covered in gold stars, and I'll wear it with my glittery pink vest. I'm going to use some old Christmas decorations to make a gold tinsel crown with gold baubles. Nolly's found an old gold curtain to make a cloak and she's going to fix on a big stand-up collar. Mum's given me a pair of old boots, which I'm decorating

127

with some sticky gold tape. And I am going to have a big gold belt. It'll be brilliant!

Miss Moody told us that she's now got a teams' rota chart drawn up. Each team of four will be made up from Years Eight, Nine and Ten. Mondays will have a team of six. Because it was our idea, we'll have first choice about which day to do. We voted to do Mondays so that we can stay together. She'll make up the rest of our team from Year Nine and Ten. She also told us that there's going to be a staff meeting on Thursday to discuss the future of the website as it's running on a trial basis and there has to be a decision about whether it's to continue or not. We couldn't believe that the school would think of shutting down the website! But Miss Moody says that although some teachers are really impressed with it, there are quite a few teachers who still need to be convinced. Jay said, *That's crazy. It's really popular! They can't do that! After all the time and work that's gone into it!* We decided to put a notice on the website asking kids to have their say and vote on whether they think it should keep going or not. Then Dan said, *We are not going to be beaten! We will fight for it to carry on!* And we all cheered!

Wednesday, 27th October
This is the notice we posted on the website.

WHAT DO YOU THINK OF THE
WHAT'S YOUR PROBLEM? WEBSITE?
At the moment, it's being run on a trial basis.
There's going to be a staff meeting on
Thursday to decide whether to
keep it — or bin it?
LET US KNOW WHAT YOU THINK!
Or just put your name below to keep it.
This does not need to be confidential.
The more names the better.
YOU CAN HELP SAVE THIS WEBSITE!

19.00 I was telling Mum and Ian how we were worried about the website and Mum said, *Well, it would be nice if you found a little more time to worry about Nolly!*

I do! I pop in to see her every day! I can't help it if I've got a busy life! Mum says she's been ringing Nolly several times a day from work to check she's OK, but she doesn't answer the phone. Nolly told Mum she'd been at her friend Bettie's but Mum knew she hadn't because she'd called Bettie too. She's definitely becoming more forgetful and confused. We all have to keep a very beady eye on her.

Thursday 28th October
16.10. Millions of messages about the

129

website today. Here are some of them.

• I don't have many problems but I think it's good for people who have.

• It really helped me. Don't let them take it away from us!

• It stops you feeling sorry for yourself when you read other peoples' problems.

• It shouldn't be up to teachers to decide. It's not for them, it's for us. We vote to keep it!

• Don't let them dump the website! It's wicked!

• It was great when I got lots of kids answering my message. I didn't feel so lonely.

• If U R getting hassle, this is the place that helps. Bullies suck. **They** should be dumped.

• Please, please, please LEAVE OUR WEBSITE ALONE.

• I wrote in at the start about having to be a carer for my mum. There are three of us now who send messages about this. It's really important to me.

17.50. Made Nolly a cup of tea and watched *Countdown* with her, when in came Mum and Ian. Went into super-helpful action and made them a cup of tea too. Ian said *Haven't you forgotten something?* I said, *Oh yeah,* and fetched the biscuit tin.

He said, *I don't mean that. Your mum's been to the hospital today, remember? She's had her first scan.* Then Mum said, *And one thing's for certain – it's not twins after all.* I was SO disappointed. Then Ian yelled, *Because it's triplets!* The printout of the scan is AMAZING! You can see three little babies, all curled up, and their heads and their little noses! They are twelve weeks old. **WOW! I'M GOING TO BE BIG SISTER TO TRIPLETS!**

Friday, 29th October
The last day in the W.Y.P office before the new rota starts.

16.30. At lunchtime, Miss Moody reported back to us about the staff-meeting decision on the website.
• Some teachers thought it wasted too much time and that teachers were here to teach, not to do social work.
• It causes too much demand and disturbance in the library at lunchtime.
• Some kids are using it to fool around.
• The school has more urgent and important needs to spend the time and money on.
• **BUT**...they voted that the website should carry on, then they should look at it again at the end of term.
    Miss Moody says she's got a couple of ideas to make sure it has a good chance of

continuing, but they're secret at the moment. Then she brought in a big cake. She said it was to thank us for starting something that we should be really proud of!

18.45. Went round to Kerry's after school. She can't stop thinking about Dan. She said, *At least you know that Jay fancies you.* I said, *I think Jay might love football more than me! He hasn't been round for ages – and we've only been out together once! Anyhow, he hasn't even kissed me yet! I thought he fancied me, but now I'm not sure.* Kerry reckons that because we spend so much time together in the office they've got used to us and take us for granted – we're more like good mates than girlfriends. She thinks that we should play more hard to get, by acting cool and strong and mysterious, like real warrior princesses, who are tough and independent, but at the same time alluring. So that's what we're going to do. Promised Kerry I'd do some research on whether Dan fancies someone else.

PLAYING HARD TO GET
Rules
1. Don't keep phoning Jay.
2. Act cool and mysterious, by doing the following:
     a) If he calls, don't rush to the phone.

b) Better still, get Mum to answer the phone and pretend I'm having a really busy exciting life.

Have written out a sheet of instructions for Mum on *What To Say To Jay* if he rings for me:

• Sorry, Jay, you've just missed her. I think she's gone round to Gareth's.

• Finch is out right now and won't be back till late — she's gone to a party.

• Oh dear, you just missed her again. She got invited to the pictures.

• Oh, you've just missed her again. She's so popular we hardly see any thing of her. Try again tomorrow.

Have stuck it on the wall by the phone.

I feel a little bit mean now. But I have to do it!

Saturday, 30th October

10.00. Warrior Princess Sleepover tonight! Kerry's coming round and we're going to try out our costumes.

11.50. Jay phoned. I rushed to the phone, then remembered. Got Mum to say, *Oh sorry Jay, you've just missed her. She's at Gareth's, I think.* Afterwards, Mum kept saying, *Oh poor Jay — I didn't like doing that.*

Feel mega-mean now. But it's the only way.

Sunday, 31st October

11.30. It was a really wicked girl-power sleepover! Sabine came as Princess Cleo, who has the power to turn into a leopard and can read minds. Sara was Princess Amethyst who can fly and rides a unicorn. Mia was Princess Marina (she was going to be Princess Neptuna – but it sounded a bit fishy), who is half-human and half-mermaid and rides dolphins. Narinder was Princess Sapphire with the powers of fire and healing. She brought some body paints. They are brilliant! We did our faces, arms and legs with them. We looked SO SCARY. Narinder painted Mia's head for her too and she looked so cool that we all wanted our heads painted. Mia said that her dad's going to do a sponsored shave to help raise money for a new scanner at the hospital. Then, Kerry said, *Wow! Why don't we all do that?* That's when we realised that we didn't really want to shave our heads. Everyone except Kerry! She seriously wants to shave her head! Mia said she could always borrow her wig if it didn't turn out right.

Sara yelled, *I've got another idea! Why don't we have a sponsored wear-a-wig day at school! We could all wear our sparkly wigs!* And Narinder said, *And people who don't have wigs could wear hats!* We're going to ask if we can do it. We made up this warrior princess rap too:

We're warrior princesses – do you hear?
Warrior princesses have no fear!
Warrior princesses give in never!
Warrior princesses stick together!
Our powers are great
Our words are true
Girls join us now
And be one too!

12.15. Mum told me that Ian heard noises downstairs last night and found Nolly with her coat over her nightie, trying to get out of the front door. She was quite cross when Mum took her back to bed. Mum's very upset about it, even though she's used to old people wandering off. At Greytiles Nursing Home where she works, old Mr Cobbold is always trying to escape. Ian's going to get an extra lock for the front door and hide the keys.

12.45. Jay phoned again! Ha ha! It's working then. He left a message for me to call him. Sor-reee! Warrior princesses DO NOT RING BACK! Our powers are great! Our words are true!

12.50. It's SO HARD being a warrior princess.

12.55. Shall I ring him? Oh, oh, oh...

13.10. Nope. Phoned Kerry instead. She's coming round.

18.20 Me and Kerry made up this wicked warrior princess rap-dance routine and showed it to Nolly. She said, *Warrior princesses, eh? Aye – that'll do me!* And joined in. Kerry's decided she doesn't want to be a skinhead after all and will wear her sparkly wig.

Monday, 1st November
16.50. Got to school early to meet up with the other warrior princesses. Jay was over by the netball posts. He waved me over, but I pretended I hadn't seen him. Then in the W.Y.P office he asked, *Who's this Gareth then?* I said, *Oh, just a mate.* He just shrugged, *Oh – right* and slouched back to his computer. I felt SO CRUEL! I nearly confessed then. But warrior princesses have to be strong. But it's working! It's working! Tee hee hee!

Narinder is going to ask Miss Moody about having a sponsored WEAR-A-WIG-OR-HAT DAY in P.S.H.E tomorrow. We went round telling everyone in our class to make sure they back it up.

21.15. Nolly's gone missing! Her telly's on – and all her lights – but there's no sign of Nolly anywhere. She was definitely there at eight o'clock because I showed her my warrior princess costume design. Mum's phoned round Nolly's friends but they haven't seen her, so Ian's gone out looking for her.

22.00. Ian couldn't find her. He's reported Nolly to the police as a missing person.

WISH 15 Please let Nolly be OK.

23.25. We just heard Nolly come in – and rushed down to the hall to find her disappearing into her flat. She was wearing a new leather bomber jacket! Mum cried, *Where have you been, Nolly!* Nolly sighed, *Oh just for a wee walk. And it's a poor thing if a person cannae slip out for a moment without being leapt upon the moment they step through their own front door, lass. And now I'll be away to my bed. Goodnight!* The jacket is a mystery.

Tuesday, 2nd November

17.45. We spent part of the P.S.H.E lesson brainstorming ideas for fund-raising for the hospital scanner. Everyone is excited about it. This is what the class wants to do.

1. Have a WEAR-A-HAT or WEAR-A-WIG day where everyone who takes part has to pay a pound.

2. Organise a YEAR-EIGHT RAVE, which would cost two pounds a ticket.

So at lunchtime all six of us went to see Mrs Enderby, Head of Year, about it. We thought she'd start on about wig-and-hat-silliness or something, but she's really keen. She says she needs to discuss it with the other Year-Eight staff first.

We told Mr Curtis about it in music. He said, *A rave eh? Well, I'm just the man!* He's offered to be the DJ! Kerry said, *It won't be a rave, no way, not in school, not with teachers around. It'll be more like a playgroup party.*

Acted cool and mysterious with Jay and Dan all day but I kept worrying about Nolly, so went to the library and sent a message to the W.Y.P site about it.

I am worried about my gran because she's getting very forgetful and confused. She wandered off the other night and is behaving strangely. Worried, Year Eight.

19.05. Kerry phoned. She's wondering if the reason that Dan isn't interested in her is because he's got a secret girfriend out of school. Said I would do some research on it.

19.10. Phoned Jay and asked him if Dan fancies anyone in particular.
He said, *Why?*

I said, *Oh, just curious.*
He said, *Do you fancy him, then?*
Would you mind if I did?
Well, yeah. You don't do you? (He minds! He minds!)
Not really. So, does Dan have a girlfriend, then?
No. Not that I know of. What's all this about?
Doesn't he fancy any one at all, then?
No – not unless you count Lara Croft.
YES! YES! Jay minds about me fancying someone else!

19.20. Phoned Kerry and told her that Dan fancies Lara Croft.

Wednesday, 3rd November

16.15. Kerry came to school with her fringe all spiky Lara-Croft style and wearing sunglasses. Until Mr Morris made her take them off. All of us – me, Kerry, Sara, Sabine, Narinder and Mia, all wore French-look sexy knee-socks today. Kerry borrowed her mum's *Givenchy* perfume so we gave ourselves a spraying in the loos at lunchtime, then Kerry donned her Lara Croft shades, then me and her sauntered over to where Jay and Dan were playing football in the playground, wafting our alluring perfume in their direction. Sara, Mia, Sabine and Narinder were killing themselves laughing.

As we filed into the classroom after the bell, Dan and Jay kept grinning and nudging each other but we played it VERY COOL.

Thursday, 4th November

16.30. The sponsored WEAR-A-WIG-OR-HAT DAY is on for Friday 19th! Also, the Year-Eight RAVE – in the evening! It's going to be a SHAVE RAVE because not only is Mr Curtis going to be the DJ – but he's going to have a sponsored shave! And he'll have his hair shaved off on the night! We've all decided to wear our warrior princess costumes. Went round to Kerry's after school and redesigned her costume. Warrior Princess Astra is going to have to look like Lara Croft now. Sara, Sabine, Narinder and Mia are going to make some posters for the Shave Rave and we're going to advertise it on the website. Mrs Enderby's going to organise some sponsor forms.

Got some answers to my email about Nolly. Some were sad, but some were really helpful.

• My granddad's like that. He has good days and bad days. Other times he's just like his old self. SL, Year Nine.

• My nan remembers lots of things from when she was young but forgets who I am sometimes, or she thinks I'm my sister. She can still beat me at draughts though. Cat lover, Year Ten.

Friday, 5th November

16.40. Jay blew me a kiss! No one saw. It was at the end of music when I went to put a drum back in the cupboard. Jay was in there already, putting the keyboards on the shelf. He turned round, smiled and blew me this kiss! So I caught it and blew it back. Then he sort of batted it back to me — so I batted it back to him. Then he dived for it — and flipped it back to me. I whacked it back again, but this time he caught it on his finger. Then he put the finger with my kiss on straight on to his lips! And kissed it! It made me go all faint! It was like **KISS PING-PONG!** It makes me go wibbly just remembering it. Kerry's dead jealous. I'm going to lie down and think about nothing else.

22.00. In bed. Can't stop thinking about Jay and kiss ping-pong...

Saturday, 6th November

9.30. Kerry phoned and invited me to go with her family to the firework display in the park tonight. They're going to pick me up at six thirty.

10.20. Jay phoned and asked if I'd like to go round to his cousin's with him for fireworks and bangers and mash. I wanna go! I wanna go! Kerry won't mind — I'll phone her!

10.30. She wailed, *Oh, you can't leave me on my own! Warrior princesses don't let each other down. I'll be completely miz on my own! We vowed to stick together and be strong.* She started giggling. *It's working though, isn't it? This playing hard to get is working!*

10.50. Phoned Jay and said I couldn't go! He sounded really fed up. I feel so mean and horrible. But Kerry's right. IT'S WORKING!

11.10. Kerry phoned. Dan had just phoned her! He asked if she'd like to go to the firework display with him! Would I mind if she went with Dan? I screamed, *WHAT! AFTER ALL YOU JUST SAID! Yeah — I DO MIND!* So she had to ring back and tell him she couldn't go after all.

12.50. I'm dead worried about Nolly. Cleaned her flat while she was out shopping with Mum — and found this carrier bag behind her chest-of-drawers. It was stuffed full of brand new expensive looking things. A huge pair of leather gloves, a pair of goggles, a clock radio, a big bag of dog biscuits, and a rubber dog-bone! Then I

remembered Cassie's granddad.
Blimey.

WORRY 19 I think Nolly's been nicking stuff!
Did she nick her leather bomber jacket too?

I've told Mum and Ian. Mum says not to
say anything to her 'cos Nolly probably
realises that she's forgetting things and it will
be frightening for her. Whatever happens we
will look after her. We have to make sure
that she doesn't go off wandering at night
again. It's so weird because sometimes Nolly's
just like her normal self and other times all
forgetful. Mum says that's how it happens. I
don't want her to go **gaga**!

16.45. Ian's fixed a new lock on the
front door and will keep the keys
with ours upstairs.

Sunday, 7th November
10.00. Fireworks were good, but
Kerry dragged me round the whole
evening searching for Dan.

12.00. Twinkle went missing. After a
big search I found her having a snooze
in my old school bag in the bottom of
my wardrobe. Then inside the front pocket I
found some old photo-booth snaps of me
and Cass. We were fooling about

and making silly faces. Suddenly I felt sad, sad, sad. It's two weeks since I left a message at her dad's and she's never phoned me or anything. Can't believe that after nine years of being best mates this would happen!

14.15. Pedalled round to Cass's house. There was a big FOR SALE sign in the garden. Where is she? What's happening? Have they moved away?

16.00. Told Mum that I'd like three girl triplets if poss. Mum would like two boys and one girl because then she'd have two boys and two girls altogether. Ian said. *Just so long as there's not just one little boy baby. Poor lad won't get a word in edgeways with three bossy sisters.* Then Mum said to me, *The problem is, Finch, where are we going to put them when they arrive? The only possibility is to use your room. Nolly says you can use her room for a bit. Then we'll have to think about looking for a bigger house.* WHAT! WHAT! I DON'T WANT TO GIVE UP MY ROOM!

Monday, 8th November
Loads of messages this morning saying SAVE OUR WEBSITE! — had 507 so far.

Started selling tickets for THE SHAVE RAVE today. There are about 180 kids in Year Eight and we've already sold seventy-nine tickets!

Forty-three have signed up for the WEAR-A-WIG-OR-HAT day and taken sponsorship forms.

Tuesday, 9th November

In geography, Kerry suddenly let rip this enormous squeal because Dan had blown a kiss to her. She didn't get a chance to catch it and blow it back because she squealed so loud that Mr Pickles glared at her and said, *Kerry Jones! What is the matter with you?*

Wednesday, 10th November

19.35. Sold loads more tickets today. Kerry came round to work on her warrior princess costume. Nolly hadn't heard of Lara Croft so we showed her a picture. She toddled off and found some old black wool and made a long thick Lara Croft plait for Kerry to clip on to her hair and I found an old tool belt of Ian's in the shed which looks just like a pair of gun holsters. Kerry's going to get some water pistols to put in them. All she needs now is shorts, fingerless gloves, and a backpack.

Thursday, 11th November

16.20. The school website is famous! And so are we! We are going to be on the local TV six o'clock news! They came to school to film us in the office. Also we were interviewed and photographed by a reporter from *The Fletchley News!* Miss Moody had secretly organised it all. It was brilliant. The only thing to spoil it was the pushy Year Nines and Tens who were acting like it was all their idea.

16.45. Phoned Ian on his mobile to tell him so he'll make sure that Mum's home in time to watch the news.

18.40. We were on telly! Well, my right ear was. And you could just about see the back of Kerry's head. They cut out loads of our interview! It was mostly Angela Big-head Harrington from Year Ten sitting at the computer waffling on. Just 'cos she's got long blond hair and big blue eyes! All you could see of Jay was his hand on the back of her chair and Dan's shoulder. The newspaper report was good, though.

WHAT'S YOUR PROBLEM?

Well, there's no problem for the kids at Finchley High School. Bright-spark Year-Eight pupils Finch Penny, Jay Carter, Dan Murphy and Kerry Jones came up with the idea of a school website where pupils can air their problems and share solutions. Teacher Miss Fiona Moody said, "Sharing problems can be a lifeline for children who have no one else to turn to. It's proving a great success. We hope we can continue."

They wouldn't bin the website after all this, would they? No.

Friday, 12th November

A hundred and twenty-two tickets have been sold for the Shave Rave so far! And we ran out of sponsor forms for the SHAVE and the WEAR-A-WIG-OR-HAT days, so we've got to print more.

Saturday, 13th November

16.45. Kerry came round and we had a dress rehearsal of our costumes. Practised our rap-dance routine too. We are fantastic! Kerry said, *Dan and Jay just won't be able to resist us now. Though they're a bit wimpy, aren't*

they? You'd have thought they'd have kissed us by now. If they don't, we'll just have to pounce on them because that's what real warrior princesses would do.
But then we decided – N⊙, because:
1. It just wouldn't be so exciting.
2. It's not very romantic.
3. Girls shouldn't have to do all the work.
Then YES, because we are warrior princesses.
Then N⊙, because warrior princesses wouldn't bother with wimps.

So we decided not to pounce.

GRAEMELLA is six weeks old today! ⊙nly three more weeks and she's mine, all mine! Told Twinkle she's to have a new friend soon. She squeaked like mad!

WARRIOR PRINCESS GRAEMELLA RAP

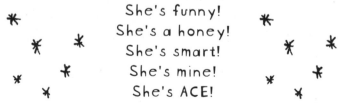

She's the princess of the bunnies
With the cutest little face.
She's funny!
She's a honey!
She's smart!
She's mine!
She's ACE!

Sunday, 14th November
The weirdest night in all our lives. Mum, me and Ian are TRULY GOBSMACKED!
I was woken up in the middle of the night

148

by that motorbike again.
Then I heard the front
door click! I looked out
of the window – and
there was Nolly, her
bomber jacket over her nightie,
toddling down the path. The motorbike was
right outside and on it was a man with a
bushy white beard and wearing a crash
helmet. He got off, took another crash helmet
from the saddle bag – and helped Nolly put it
on! Next thing, she climbed on to the back of
the motorbike – and they roared off into the
night together! They had matching jackets and
helmets! I rushed upstairs and woke Mum and
Ian. They thought I must have been dreaming
until they found her empty bed. Ian couldn't
understand how she's got the key to the new
lock, so he checked our kitchen drawer – and
there was one key missing! Nolly must have
nicked it! Mum said, *There's something funny
going on here. Nolly's not as daft as she's
pretending. What's she up to?*

We waited up all night, dozing on the sofa.
Then, at about six o'clock, we heard the
motorbike again. We peeped out from behind
the curtain – and there they were. The man
helped Nolly climb off – then they went into
this great passionate clinch! We all rushed
out in our dressing gowns, Mum calling,
Where have you been, Nolly? Don't you know

= vroom

how worried we've been! They looked a bit startled, then the man said, *Looks like we've been rumbled, Olive.* (That's her real name.) Nolly nodded, *Aye, we've been caught red-handed. Well, we'd better go inside and tell them then, hadn't we?* So we all went in and Nolly said, *This is my friend – boyfriend – Bill.* We all just gawped. Nolly laughed, *Ye dinnae have to look so shocked – I may be seventy-three on the outside, but inside I feel seventeen! Aye, I haven't had so much fun in years. And Bill has asked me to marry him!* Then Bill said, *So we hope you'll be happy for us and give us your blessing.*

Mum and me started blubbing then – with happiness for Nolly, and sadness that she's going to leave us! Ian's eyes went watery as well. Nolly met Biker Bill in hospital. That's who she's been sneaking out to see on all these mystery disappearances. He's a line-dancer too. Nolly has asked Mum and me to be bridesmaids and Ian to be best man. After they're married, she's going to move in with Bill in his retirement flat. Biker Bill is seventy-five next week and he's got a dog called Buster. That's what all that stuff in the carrier bags was for! Nolly's not a bit gaga – and I'm going to have a granddad!

Monday, 15th November
16.20. Had hardly any sleep last night and

couldn't concentrate at all in
school today. Kept thinking
about Nolly and Biker Bill. Kerry
said, *What! They were actually
SNOGGING?* I said I didn't want
to think about that. I kept
getting pictures in my head of false
teeth clonking together. She asked, *Do you
think they were having — you know,
SLEEPOVERS?* I was going, *Don't! Don't even
talk about it. They wouldn't, would they? Not
at their age. They probably just have cuddles.*

Tuesday, 16th November

17.00. Dee-dah! The website is saved! Miss
Moody told us that the staff meeting voted
for it to carry on to the end of the school
year, when it will be reviewed. We only do
one session a week now and it's great having
our lunch breaks back. We've been using one
of the music practice rooms to rehearse our
warrior princess routine.

21.10. Bill's been here all evening. He's
travelled all over America on his motorbike!
The wedding will be on Saturday, 10th
December, then they're going on a honeymoon
to Majorca, and Nolly will be letting the
house to us. So we'll have plenty of room for
the triplets after all. Mum's bump is really
showing now. She's stopped feeling sick — and

now can't stop eating. She's going to get ENORMOUS with three babies in there. I'm starting to think that maybe Mum and Ian ought to be thinking of getting married. If they REALLY love each other they should. Has Ian asked her? If not, why not? I'm going to drop some BIG HINTS. They could have a DOUBLE WEDDING! With Nolly and Bill!

21.55. Just had a strange thought. By the time the triplets are my age I'LL BE NEARLY 25! That's ANCIENT! I could have a baby of my own by then! And the triplets would be their aunties or uncles. Wow. THAT IS SO WEIRD!

Wednesday, 17th November
17.40. On my way back home from school I started to think about Cass again. Tried calling at her house but there was no answer, so I ripped a page out of my rough book and wrote:

> VERY IMPORTANT QUESTIONNAIRE.
> PLEASE COMPLETE AND
> RETURN A.S.A.P to Finch Penny.
> ARE WE STILL FRIENDS? Please tick...
> YES   or   NO

Sign here . . . .

Date . . . .

I MISS YOU! Where are you, Cass? Hope you're OK.
Lots and lots of luv, Finch

Then I stuck it through the letter box. Just as I reached the gate, I heard someone shout, *Hey! Finch!* And there was Cass! She said she hadn't answered the door because she thought I was Olly – who she's chucked, but still keeps calling round. (She says he was mega boring.) We went up to her room. Cass said, *Do you really miss me?* So I said, *Yeah! Of course I do!*

Oh, I didn't think you did – it didn't seem like it.

I couldn't believe it. I went, *What!*

Well, you were going round with Kay and Kerry and Dan – I felt really left out.

I said, *Well, what about when I met you at Cosmo's? You were going on about the Gothic Girls, and Olly! And you kept nattering on your mobile! I felt totally left out too! And what about all those messages I left for you? Why didn't you call back?*

Cass said, *I couldn't help it! Mum kept taking us to our nan's – and there was too much stuff happening with Mum and Dad!*

It went on like that for quite a bit. So I said, *Look, Cass, do you want to be friends or not?*

She bellowed, *NO! I DO NOT! I HATE YOU!*

I HATE YOU! And she grabbed her Miss Piggy and started bashing me with it. Then we fell about laughing. She grabbed the questionnaire and ticked the box for YES WE ARE STILL FRIENDS. And underneath wrote, FRIENDS FOR EVER! WHATEVER! *We promise to meet or phone at least once a week NO MATTER WHAT!* And we both signed it. I was there for ages! There was so much we had to catch up with. She and her mum and Leo are moving to a smaller house in Melrose Road – and that's only five minutes away from me.

Thursday, 18th November

16.00. It looks like nearly all of Year Eight are coming to the rave! We reckon we'll raise at least five hundred pounds. Going round to Sabine's for a final warrior princess dress and make-up rehearsal. I'm feeling SO nervous now!

18.40. We all looked FANTASTIC! Narinder painted Mia's head in gold and silver and she looked AMAZING. Came home in my costume to show Mum and Nolly. Mum went all dopey and said I looked beautiful. Nolly said, *Aye, you're a bonny lass. And we're all very proud of you.* Then Ian said, *Yeah, me too, Finch. Real proud.*

Just think, said Nolly, *it was only the three of us six months ago. And now we're going to be a family of five.* Ian patted Mum's tum and grinned. *No, Nolly,* he said, *eight, remember?*

21.30. WISH 16 I wish that Jay kisses me.

Friday, 19th November
22.40. The most WONDERFUL NIGHT OF MY LIFE. The warrior princesses were the best ever! All the girls joined in our chant and dance — and Miss Moody, Mrs Enderby, Miss Parkes and Mrs Truman — all chanting and stomping. All the time I could feel Jay watching me. Afterwards, he came over and started dancing with me. He put his arms round me and we sort of smooched — except you can't really smooch with teachers around, so we went outside to get some fresh air. It was dark by then and the stars were all twinkly-twinkly. And then...
he kissed me
he kissed me
he kissed me
he kissed me
he kissed me
he kissed me...

ORCHARD BOOKS
96 Leonard Street, London EC2A 4XD
Orchard Books Australia
32/45-51 Huntley Street, Alexandria, NSW 2015
First published in Great Britain in 2003
A paperback original
Text © Pat Moon 2003
Illustrations © Sarah Nayler 2003
A CIP catalogue record for this book is available from the British Library.
ISBN 1 84121 456 6
1 3 5 7 9 10 8 6 4 2
Printed and bound in China

If you've enjoyed reading
Finch's Top Secrets
as revealed only to Pat Moon, you may
also enjoy these books by Pat Moon:

ORCHARD RED APPLES

Do Not Read this Book
Shortlisted for the
SHEFFIELD CHILDREN'S BOOK AWARD
Pick of the Year
CHILDREN'S BOOK AWARD

ORCHARD BLACK APPLES

The Spying Game
Shortlisted for the
GUARDIAN CHILDREN'S FICTION AWARD
and the WRITERS' GUILD AWARD

Double Image
Shortlisted for the
SMARTIES BOOK PRIZE

Nathan's Switch

The Ghost of Sadie Kimber

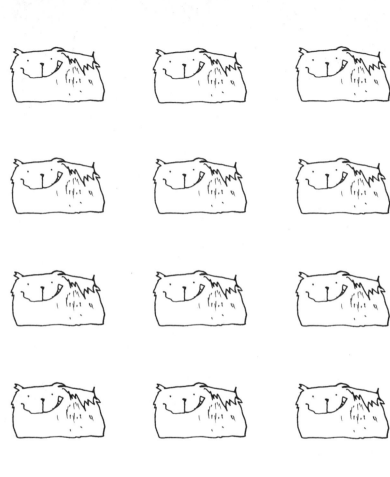

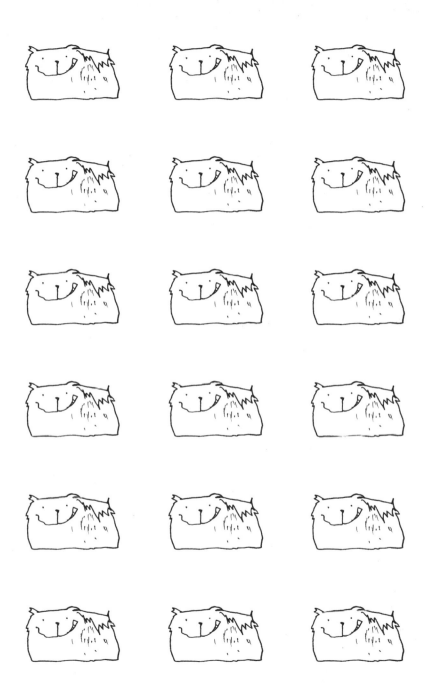